OVERWATCH 2
SOJOURN

T0333279

Also available from Titan Books

Overwatch: The Official Cookbook
The Cinematic Art of Overwatch: Volume 1
The Cinematic Art of Overwatch: Volume 2
The Overwatch Short Story Collection

OVERWATCH 2
SOJOURN

TEMI OH

TITAN BOOKS

Overwatch 2: Sojourn
Print edition ISBN: 9781803364506

Published by Titan Books
A division of Titan Publishing Group Ltd
144 Southwark Street, London SE1 0UP
www.titanbooks.com

First edition: November 2022
10 9 8 7 6 5 4 3 2 1

This is a work of fiction. All of the characters, organizations, and events portrayed in this novel are either products of the author's imagination or are used fictitiously. Any resemblance to actual persons, living or dead (except for satirical purposes), is entirely coincidental.

A CIP catalogue record for this title is available from the British Library.

Printed and bound by CPI Group (UK) Ltd, Croydon CR0 4YY.

PROLOGUE

Her father liked to say that she was born twice. The second time, in that Toronto hospital, in a body rebuilt. New discs in her spine. Her chest, a titanium cage. Heart, a silicone fist, pounding inside.

Sometimes, on the edge of waking, Vivian Chase thinks she can hear his voice, and her mother's and Valentine's, the shout of joy they all made when she came back to them.

"Human or omnic?"

This time, the voice that pries her consciousness open is unfamiliar.

"Sorry?" she says. She wakes horribly, her skull full of razor wire. Bones sore, the bruised skin on her temple—where she's been hit—throbbing.

The world comes spinning into view.

"Where am I?" Chase asks.

She's lying on grass, and a scanner floats above her head, the voice from its speakers ringing in a tinny monotone. It's the kind of tech she's used to seeing at airport security or at the front doors of shopping centers.

"I'm not equipped to answer your question," the scanner says.

"Right," Chase mutters, pulling herself up on her elbows. When she was knocked out, she was on Centre Island, part of the small chain of islands in Lake Ontario. She can tell from the trees around her that she has not moved very far. And from here, she can see Toronto's skyline lit carmine, she thinks at first with sunset but then, Chase realizes, with flames.

What is she doing here? Memories are beginning to float back on a cresting wave of panic. A plane fell out of the sky. The power stopped. The last thing she recalls is the omnic attack. Shouts of violence. Terrified screams. Her niece, her sister—

"*Valentine!*" she shouts now, searching frantically. She was trying to save Valentine.

"This is a holding bay," the scanner says. It's an area about the size of a basketball court, surrounded by plexiglass walls. All around her are decommissioned omnics, humanoid robots with the Omnica Corp logo branded on their metallic hulls. Some of them are dented and in pieces, sparks from frayed wires winking at her. Others are slumped like drunks on the edge of the bay, or riddled with bullet holes, piled on top of each other like a litter of sleeping dogs.

Something terrible is happening. Even from where Chase is sitting now, the back of her throat burns with the acrid tang of smoke and some industrial smell, like scorched metal. The sound of gunfire tears the air, and beneath it distant shouts, cries of alarm, pain, the thunder of boots. It's as if she's on the periphery of a battlefield: sirens wail somewhere, engines roar. Terror makes her chest tight. Valentine and Chase's niece, Bonnie, are nowhere to be seen.

"I need to get out," she shouts at the scanner. Getting shakily to her feet, Chase examines the wall of the holding bay. There's an electric field in front of it, she can tell without touching it, something about the almost subsonic hum it's making. "I need to find them," she says, more to herself than the scanner. "I need to make sure they're okay."

"I'm not authorized to release any omnics," it says.

With a flash of annoyance that Chase works hard to keep back, she says, "I'm clearly human."

The scanner activates once more, and a laser appears, sliding up then down her body before it emits an ear-piercing howl.

"I am not authorized to release any omnics," the scanner repeats.

The machine is probably responding to the high level of synthetic compounds in her body. Her artificial heart renders her pulse almost undetectable, and the cybernetics in her head and eyes often trigger security scanners.

It feels absurd to her, in this moment, that she must disclose her medical history to this tin can of a machine. Especially when, somewhere out there, her sister and niece could be in danger.

Breathing deeply, Chase explains it the way she has a thousand times. "I have a condition—an autoimmune disease. My spine, heart, lungs, and most of my bones were replaced with cybernetics in a medical procedure. I can prove it—"

"I'm not authorized to release any omnics," the scanner repeats.

"Augh!" Chase shouts in frustration, fighting the urge to slam a fist into its monitor screen. "Can I just talk to a human?"

"Chase? Vivian Chase?"

Chase turns to find a shadow emerging from the trees. Major Campbell, a man she hasn't seen since her early days in infantry. Some four years on, his height and barrel chest still make him look larger than life. But the years have left some marks—a bald head and a graying stubble, blue eyes that flash like a cat's in the gloom.

"What is it now? Sergeant? Captain?"

"Not yet," she says.

"Our records show you're on leave," he says, slowing as he reaches the perimeter of the holding bay.

"I was, sir." Then she corrects herself. "I am. I was on Centre Island when—"

How to describe what happened? The day was calm and bright, and then . . . the park erupted into terrified chaos.

Campbell's face is grave. "It's a mess out there, Chase."

That morning, Vivian Chase and Valentine couldn't have guessed at the disaster awaiting them when they ventured out to the theme park with Valentine's five-year-old daughter, Bonnie.

It was a happy homecoming for Chase, a joy to return to the neighborhood she'd grown up in and to this place, the Centre

Island amusement park, that their parents had loved to take them.

"It feels like nothing's changed," she says to her sister as Bonnie makes one more round on the Beastly Bears ride. Just the sight of the child makes her think of Valentine at that age: gap-toothed, her hair tied up in cotton-candy Afro puffs, sitting happily in the embrace of the coverall-clad bears. This is like Chase's childhood too: watching from the sidelines as the joyful shouts of children peal out across the sky. She was almost always too sick to join in whatever fun her sister was having, or her parents were too overcautious to let her.

"Some things have changed," Valentine says slightly defensively. She nods at the ticket booths and the park rangers—everything is operated by omnics now and not bored teenagers. Bonnie has one too, an omnic caretaker dressed like an English nanny, backlit visual sensors positioned in its head like eyes and a periwinkle dress with a Peter Pan collar. She speaks in a singsong register that feels a little creepy to Chase, though Bonnie seems to love her. The little girl begged Valentine to pay for the two of them to get on a ride together.

"I don't understand why the omnic needs a ticket as well," Chase says, taking a sip of the big blue slushy she ordered at the concession stand.

"Well, she's taking up a seat on the ride," Valentine says, waving as Bonnie and the omnic turn the right-hand corner. "And . . . I don't know. Having an omnic . . . they sort of become part of the family after a while. The technology has advanced a lot since your days with Grandpa's old VAC model."

"Even with Omnica shut down?"

"Oh, there are lots of companies filling that void. Omnica's whole problem was that they were pushing the technology a little *too* far. Didn't you hear about that scientist there? The one who built Aurora. What was her name?" Valentine snaps a finger.

"Liao," Chase says, though the story still makes her feel a little uneasy. "I heard her work on Aurora was just an aberration, though, something they couldn't mass-produce. And now the UN has put limits on that kind of research."

"Sure, maybe," Valentine says. "But it's funny living with an omnic—they do start to seem alive to you after a while."

"They still make me nervous," Chase says.

Valentine touches her sister's arm. "Or is it that they make you uncomfortable because some of their tech is in your legs?"

Chase kicks at the ground but stays quiet. She has always been grateful for the technology that saved her life. Truth be told, she's relished the strength and speed of her cybernetic legs, even if it only gives her a slight edge over her comrades. But being in the military—in a career that celebrates physical uniformity—it can be complicated having a body that is different, that sometimes needs specialized care. She doesn't like to draw attention to it. And she really doesn't like the idea of being lumped in with robots just because they share some technology.

"What I know?" Valentine says. "Their technology was part of what saved your life. And honestly, Julietta is giving me a whole new lease on mine." That's what Bonnie named the nanny omnic Valentine and her husband took out a small loan to buy. "You have no idea what it was like before her . . . Getting home from work, exhausted, having to chase my kid around, or throw some leftovers together, collapsing on the sofa at her bedtime, and still the house was a mess. Our daycare and takeout budget alone was higher than the mortgage. Now I come home and everything is *clean*, taken care of . . ." Valentine casts a loving gaze in Julietta's direction. "I got pregnant with her so young. I thought I'd never be able to get back to finishing my degree. There was just no way I could achieve any of my ambitions with all the responsibilities I needed to balance. But now . . ."

The Toronto skyline is only a little different from her memory, more crowded than before, buildings jostling like loose teeth against the blue. There, the CN Tower, Scotia Plaza, and, among them, impressive structures she doesn't recognize—luxury condominiums and newer shopping centers—and one she does, one of Omnica's former offices, its glass facade glittering like a knife in the afternoon sun.

"Too bad Omnica isn't around for your glowing review," Chase says. Creating Aurora was the beginning of the end for the company. Divided everyone involved, sent them into a tailspin, opened them up to a huge amount of scrutiny they weren't able to withstand. "Though, it still feels like the robots are everywhere." Chase read that there's now one omnic for every eight humans in Canada.

"Because they make our lives *better*," says Valentine. "I bet if you got one—"

"I don't *want* one," Chase says, though it comes out sounding firmer than she intended. They're quiet for a little while. A kid vomits her cherry-flavored slushy all over her clothes and waddles to her mother with tears in her eyes. Her robot nanny stands ready with a change of clothes. An omnic caretaker helps an old man up from a bench, and they smile at each other.

Hard to deny all the good the robots are doing, Chase thinks. Beyond the cybernetics that saved Chase's life, she came of age just as countries began to adopt all kinds of new technology— systems that linked to local traffic and weather systems, governed school boards, and allocated resources to hospitals. Major AIs that helped design improvements to the economy, agriculture, global communication, as well as leading innovations in ecological preservation. Chase knows it would be irrational to complain about the robots without acknowledging the fact that the world they live in now is far better than the one she grew up in and is getting even better every day. Bonnie can expect to live decades longer than someone born a generation ago. Her education will be perfectly tailored to her interests and needs, and she will grow up in a world where there is less global conflict than before.

Aurora had called all that good into question though—had made society stop and ask if maybe they'd gone too far. Chase had undoubtedly benefited from many of Omnica's advancements, but she also believed some scientific doors were best left unopened. Which is perhaps why she's still not spending her money on a robot assistant.

"I wish you'd come back more often," Valentine says.

"I want to—" A pang of guilt twists in Chase's stomach.

It's been a year since they last saw each other. Bonnie seems to be twice her former size, and easily twice as clever. Valentine is the same, though. Even before Chase's sickness, no one could ever guess the two of them were twins. Chase's features look different somehow on Valentine's softly made-up face. Deep-set eyes, high cheekbones, and cherrywood skin. Valentine leans over now to take a sip from Chase's slushy. When she smiles, her lips, teeth, and tongue are stained cobalt.

"I thought we'd grow up together, settle down back here. Maybe our children would be friends."

"Thought or hoped?" Chase shrugs. "There's not only one kind of life."

The music stops on the bear ride, and Julietta helps to unlatch Bonnie's safety harness.

Growing up with parents in the Canadian military, Chase and Valentine were used to traveling around. They moved all over Canada and even spent a couple of months in London, Dubai, and many parts of the United States. Chase loved the travel, loved learning about new places and cultures, other histories. Valentine, though, always hated it. Cried for weeks whenever she discovered they were leaving. When they said goodbye to their home in Ontario, she went carefully about the empty rooms touching the lintels of the doors, floorboards, and windowsills, bidding farewell to everything.

It came as little surprise to Chase that just a year after Valentine graduated from high school, she married her boyfriend and settled down in the suburbs of Toronto.

"Maybe you're just more of a homebody and I'm more of an—"

"Adventurer?" Valentine says.

Chase smiles. She often wonders if they've always been

different or if her illness made her different. While Chase was in the hospital or following her mother from one specialist appointment to another, Valentine enjoyed a relatively ordinary adolescence, hanging out with her friends and winning medals for their school swim team. Maybe those early years of feeling confined by her body and circumstance are the reason that Chase relishes her freedom so much now. Enjoys every deployment with the CAF and every opportunity to meet new people or learn new things. If their situations were reversed . . . would Chase have chosen something different? This happy domesticity? A voice inside tells her no, that somehow she was always destined for this life. But she had little doubt that everything she went through had solidified this direction for her, and gave her the tools to make her better suited for it.

Bonnie races up to them, all excited chatter and giggles, begging her mother for one more ride, but Valentine is already frowning and checking the time. "We made reservations for lunch—"

"Just one more, Mama, please?" Bonnie points to the swan ride. Valentine relents quickly, and they head to the edge of the lake to watch as Bonnie and her nanny omnic begin to make their leisurely way around the water on the big swan-shaped boats.

The first sign of disaster is the plane. It catches everyone's attention because it's flying too low. It swings under the clouds with an ominous squeal of mechanics, like a howl of distress. Plumes of black smoke fan in its wake.

"Is that—?" Valentine shades her eyes to stare up at it, but her thought is cut short as the plane careens toward the ground and then, with a horrendous noise, crashes like a cannonball on the far end of the island.

Everyone feels the impact under their feet, in the rumble of the earth, and when they look up, all the rides have stopped. The Ferris wheel, the bumper cars, and the flume ride, the jangly music from the antique carousel. The silence is like a collective inhale, the moment before the pendulum drops back and the entire park erupts in chaos.

Right next to her, Chase notices that the old man who had been walking across the park with his omnic assistant is crying out in terror. The omnic caretaker's sensors flash and it turns on him, pushing the man to the ground so hard he shouts in pain.

Almost without thinking, Chase tosses her slushy away and rushes to the man's aid, pushing the omnic over. Its reflexes, though, are whippet-fast. It grabs the man's walking stick and takes a violent swing at her head. Her cybernetic limbs make her reflexes a couple of milliseconds faster too, and she sees it coming.

Ducking away from the blow, Chase uses the machine's momentum against it when she grabs the other end of the cane and sends the omnic flying. With a hiss of hydraulics, it's back up like a jack-in-the-box. Leaping through the sky, it brings the cane down so hard where Chase was standing that the wood splinters and the pavement cracks under the omnic's feet.

Chase hurls herself at the caretaker one more time. It loses its balance, and she comes again at the omnic's heels with another kick that sends it reeling over the guardrails and into the lake. Chase rushes to the old man and helps him onto the bench.

When she looks around, it's like waking into a nightmare. There is chaos everywhere. Omnics are leaping over concession stands to attack tourists. An omnic dog walker has let its pack loose and is chasing down a picnicking family. The park rangers are plowing a maintenance truck into a fleeing crowd. A group of teens who had been playing cricket on the grass abandons their game and tries to escape by climbing a tree.

"Valentine!" Chase shouts. Her sister is on the ground, and an omnic in a waiter's uniform is kicking her.

"Get Bonnie," Valentine sputters, but Chase barely hears her over the blood that rushes through her ears at the sight of her sister in trouble. She leaps over the upturned trash can and runs to save Valentine.

"The nanny," her sister shouts. "Go get Bonnie—save her!"

But Chase launches herself at the omnic and throws it onto the ground. The position lends her a moment of advantage, which she presses by stamping her foot down on its chest. She feels a crack in its outer casing before her heel meets some of the delicate mechanics inside. She slams her foot down again, hoping to break something, but it grabs her ankle in its fists.

Although her cybernetic enhancements make her stronger than most humans, she's still not as strong as most omnics, and it overpowers her quickly, throwing her to the grass with a force that knocks all the oxygen from her chest. Is she imagining the brightness in its eyes as it mimics her attack, kicking her hard in the sternum?

She needs a weapon. As it is, the omnic is overpowering her. It brings the heel of its foot down again on her throat and her vision blackens. She is struck again, this time on her face in a move that would have killed her sister. Metal against metal. Chase thinks of her father's aluminum baseball bat against the wall of a cage. The flesh on the side of her face erupts under the impact of the omnic's foot, and her mouth fills with blood. A blow to her head, and then another, makes starbursts of pain explode behind her eyes. The taste of cold iron under her tongue, her vision beginning to flicker. Chase scrunches protectively on her side and thinks, *It could kill me.*

But then, the sound of footsteps pounding the path. "Vivian!" A shout from her sister, who swings a cricket bat at the omnic. It's enough to throw it off-balance for a second, which gives Chase enough time to stagger to her feet, spitting blood on the grass.

Valentine takes another swing at the robot's head—as if she's trying to smash an antique television—and before it can turn to retaliate, Chase runs, using her momentum to pitch it into the lake. It falls with a mighty *crash*, and Chase reels, her body gripped with pain.

But there's another scream in the distance now.

"Bonnie!" Valentine shouts again. Her daughter has been knocked into the lake and is flailing now, struggling to keep afloat, terror in her eyes as her nannybot calmly pushes her under the water.

Chase takes two steps toward her niece, but all the blood is rushing from her head, and the sounds of the fray take on a discordant howl. Before she knows it, her body hits the gravel, and the world vanishes.

Back in the holding bay, Major Campbell explains that the army was quickly deployed to battle the rogue omnics and rescue as many civilians as possible.

"You were lucky," he tells her, although, trapped in this holding bay she woke up in, Chase feels anything but. "On this island they were easier to contain, but out there—" He nods ominously toward Toronto's burning skyline.

"Can you let me out?" Chase says. A flash of irritation creeps into her voice as she notices some hesitation in Campbell's demeanor.

"I don't understand why I'm still here," Chase says, pointing to the scanner on the wall, its rudimentary AI, "or why you're leaving it up to robots to decide who is a robot."

"They're right most of the time."

Chase grits her teeth, leaning as close to the fence as she dares. "Except, crucially, when they're not."

In the moment of tense silence between the two of them, Chase wonders if the rumors are true. She's heard that Major Campbell has expressed concern about cybernetic soldiers in the military. There is some luddite streak in his attitude, from the sound of it, that makes him suspicious of a lot of new technology, wary about relying on it, about the cost of maintaining it and the hypothetical risk of it failing at a crucial moment. In spite of the fact that un-augmented soldiers are known to be more injury prone. He has always been perfectly polite to her, but Chase wonders now if she is imagining the new chilliness in his manner.

In another moment, though, he lifts his hand to the scanner's outward-facing fingerprint pad. In a bright tone it says, "Authorization accepted," and the scanner beeps, the holding bay's electric field temporarily powering down. Once it slides open, Chase walks through.

"I lost track of my sister and my niece in the attack," she tells him. "I need to find out if they're okay."

"Most of the civilians were taken to Hanlan's Point Beach. They've set up a field hospital there."

He eyes her forehead, and Chase can only imagine the mess the omnic made of her face. The swelling, bruising, and possibly exposed metal where the omnic kicked her. Pain throbs through her skull, and blood has dried in a sticky crust down the side of her face and lips.

"Maybe a medic can check out your wounds, or"—he pauses to glance at the scratched metal on her cybernetic legs—"I don't know—a *mechanic*."

Chase bristles at this comment but doesn't say anything. The wind picks up as she limps after him across the island.

It's a war zone, she thinks. A frightening sight. As the two of them head over the pedestrian bridge on the south side of the island, Chase catches an expansive view of Toronto Harbor, where the sky is on fire, plumes of smoke obscure the tops of buildings, and explosions flash across and shatter their glass facades.

"Is it happening everywhere? The fighting? The robots?" she asks. "Do they know what's causing it?"

"Started in Lagos," Campbell says, tears stinging his eyes from the smoke. "Omnics attacking their owners. But the next wave of assaults were in tandem: London, Mexico City, Hong Kong. Like a switch flipped. Turning on families, people they've served for years—even children. We can't know the true numbers, but we estimate casualties in the millions."

The thought is baffling, that this could happen at all, and even then at such a scale.

"Fighting in the city is almost impossible," Campbell says. "It poses all the classic challenges of urban warfare—"

"Countless places for the insurgents to hide, making it difficult to establish a perimeter." Chase lists the reasons almost reflexively. "And in downtown Toronto—"

"The collateral damage will be unthinkable. Not to mention that the CAF is massively outnumbered." Words that send a chill through Chase's body as she recalls the conversation with her sister, one omnic to every eight humans. An unthinkable number for an enemy force. Campbell explains how the military managed to dismantle a lot of the omnics on Centre Island and set up a base that will be easy to defend. "We've assembled field hospitals on the surrounding islands, and at the moment we've focused our resources on evacuating the city."

Chase looks back at the smoke-darkened skyline, suddenly concerned for the well-being of her comrades who are probably fighting on the mainland right now. She only said goodbye to them a couple of days ago, before her leave commenced.

"It's not going to be easy," Campbell says. "Fighting against an enemy that doesn't eat, doesn't sleep . . . presumably *learns* from us. We might as well have handed the world over when we brought those tin cans into our lives."

Campbell's words fill Chase with dread as they move past the wreckage of the amusement park. Strange to see this place in the quiet gloom. No music playing in a canon over the speakers. No children laughing. The charred and dented rides, abandoned swan boats floating upturned in the lake, battered concession stands. Blood and grease spill like tar across the cobble path. Chase almost steps in the remains of her melted slushy, electric-blue syrup that sticks like scum to the pavement.

Chase's eyes notice something flash in the grass. She turns to pick it up and finds it's Valentine's wedding ring. It was a gift from their grandmother; it's missing one of its biggest stones. *She must have lost it in the chaos,* Chase thinks distantly, clutching it tight in a fist and working hard to hide her mounting panic from Campbell.

The two of them quickly round the corner at Hanlan's Point Beach. As children, Chase and her sister always giggled at the mention of the island's famous "clothing-optional" beach. As she and Campbell march through the brush, past sand dunes, Chase is forced to confront the scene before her with memories of beachgoers starting up a barbecue or blasting music from under bright umbrellas. In truth, though, Chase has always hated the beach—sand, salt water, and wave-battered shingle have never agreed with her cybernetics.

Tonight, massive military-grade canvas tents are pitched all along it, lamps and spotlights illuminating the gathering darkness. The spectral shadows of patients, soldiers, and army medics bob like puppets across the tarpaulin. A long fleet of military boats is moored in the lake, and all around, people are shouting orders or running to carry them out.

"You can ask Lieutenant Brady about your family." Campbell nods to a man holding a clipboard.

"Back to the Stone Age," he says, holding up a paper list with civilians' names handwritten under various holding bays. "Sorry. Our comms are a little sluggish at the moment."

"We're doing what we can," Campbell says. Then, to Chase, "All our systems have gone offline while tech works to quarantine military-grade omnics from our network."

"Is my sister's name there? Valentine Chase-Chapman? Or, um . . . Bonnie?" She is holding her breath as he flips through the pages, squinting down at the names for what feels like an excruciatingly long time. Catastrophic thoughts cross Chase's mind.

They haven't made it.

Their bodies are on stretchers somewhere.

Or lying on a beach.

And then—finally—"Bonnie," he says. "She's in critical care. That tent, can you see . . . ?" Brady points to it. The words make Chase feel dizzy, sick. She bolts in the direction that he pointed, her heart pounding. All the while she thinks about how Bonnie looked. Flailing in the lake against her nanny's metal grip.

The hastily constructed field hospital with its long ranks of makeshift beds is frightening to behold. People she saw earlier that day lie groaning in pain, blood-spattered or gravely pale. The picnickers, the kids playing cricket. A couple have died—a blanket is thrown over their still bodies.

"Bonnie," Chase says, her voice hollow with dread, and then louder, "Bonnie?"

"Viv?"

Relief floods her at the sound of her sister's voice. She's a couple of meters from her, leaning over a stretcher.

"Valentine." Chase rushes over to hug her sister but is surprised when Valentine pushes her away. In the flickering light of the ward, Chase can see that Valentine has been crying. Her face is swollen and bruised.

"Are you okay?" Chase asks. "Is Bonnie?"

She doesn't look okay. The little girl is unconscious, attached to a respirator, her chest rising and falling with the even rhythm of the machine.

"Her heart stopped," Valentine says, her eyes fixed on her daughter. "They can't say for how long." It's beating with a shallow rhythm now, Chase can see. Underneath the thin sheet, the little girl is still wearing a pinafore and a shirt with a Peter Pan collar, dressed to match her omnic nanny.

"Will she be okay?" Chase asks.

Valentine is trying not to cry.

"She's stable now, but they're saying it's touch and go."

This is better news than Chase hoped for. From what Campbell was saying, millions of people died today, or will die as this event unfolds. They survived the first attack and might live to see another day. In wartime, that's often the best victory one can ask for, as far as Chase is concerned.

But Valentine's eyes narrow, glittering with rage. "Why didn't you save her, Viv?"

It comes back to Chase as it was, the way Valentine looked, crumpled on the ground, being kicked half to death by the omnic waiter.

"It would have killed you," Chase says. She doesn't add *I saved your life.*

"I would have gladly died while you saved her. *Her heart stopped.* She—" Her sister's words are hoarse with pain.

Valentine's scream comes back to Chase. The way she pleaded, *Get Bonnie.* And even now, Chase can't explain why she didn't. Except that nothing in her would have allowed her to turn away from her twin in that moment, to abandon Valentine when the omnic was a few blows from killing her. Her panic caused her to lose sight of Bonnie in the chaos. She loves them both, but her brain did a cold calculus in that split second—to save the one she knew she could.

In an ideal world, she could have saved them both. In an ideal world, none of this would have happened. They would have watched Bonnie play on the swan ride, they'd have sipped slushies and gone for lunch and napped on the sofa in front of afternoon cartoons in Valentine's living room before her husband returned to cook them dinner.

"I'm sorry" is all she can say, ashamed and defeated. "My training must've—"

Valentine cries out again—a terrible sound Chase didn't know her sister was capable of making. She shakes now, in her grief and rage. "*Your training?* Your training would have saved me, just so I can bury my baby? How can you say that and claim to have a real heart?"

"Real?" Chase repeats, her sister's words like a punch in the solar plexus.

But Valentine keeps talking. "Leave. Please. Just . . . leave me."

A little while later, Chase is standing by the edge of Lake Ontario watching the black waves hurl themselves relentlessly against the beach. Wet air peels up off the long surf, the whole thing wind-tossed and wretched. The way she feels.

Reaching into her pocket, her fingers find Valentine's ring. She forgot to return it, but now she can't imagine facing her sister again. Chase is used to brushing the hurt away, but Valentine's words cut her deeply. They remind her of the cruel things that kids at school used to say.

After her first operation, Chase was grateful that her cybernetics allowed her to return to school. But rumors began to circulate about her. The friends she had from before her illness had moved on, now distant and wary of her. Other kids would pinch her without her permission and ask if she could feel it. Everything in their manner reminded her of her other-ness. Their too-long stares, their whispers. When someone had said that she couldn't love because she didn't have a "real" heart, Chase had sat in the bathroom and cried. Valentine had defended her, got into fights on her behalf when people called her sister names. But now...

It was her grief talking back there, Chase tells herself, and tries to believe it.

The sound of footsteps coming up the shingle draws her from her thoughts. She puts the ring back in her pocket and turns to find that it's Campbell again, and he's been looking for her.

"I hear you want to put in a request to end your leave early and return to active duty."

"Yes, sir," Chase says.

"Well, your request is approved, since CAF has just recalled all officers to active duty. And"—he takes a deep breath—"effective immediately, you're being transferred to special forces, CANSOFCOM-CSOR, and being promoted to captain."

"What?" Normally she would be elated at this news—she's been working at making captain for the better part of a year—but her mind keeps floating back to her sister, bent over Bonnie's still body.

She couldn't protect them today, but she'll ensure it's a mistake she doesn't repeat.

She collects herself. "Thank you, sir. I'm very—"

"Don't thank me," Campbell interrupts. "The promotion was automatic for soldiers with four years of active service. The CAF lost five percent of its troops in the last twelve hours. Who knows?" His eyes float up to the gathering clouds. "If you survive another twelve, you might be making my rank."

1

UNDERGROUND CITY—THREE MONTHS LATER

In some places—bombed out and razed to rubble—it can seem as if it's been years since the Omnic Crisis began. In others, like this stretch of the Underground City that Chase is now running through, it's almost as if it never happened.

Sometimes Chase herself forgets what the world was like during peacetime. But then she'll dream of going to the grocery store, or the popcorn-smelling blackness of the cinema, the foamy rosette on the top of a latte. She'll think of Valentine, of having a teddy bear picnic with Bonnie, and that old life will feel impossibly far away. Other times, though, she'll open her eyes in her bunk in the CAF's Laurentian Mountain base and for a few dreamlike seconds it will be as if the past three months were a distant nightmare.

Campbell was right. Chase returned to active duty to discover that she had been promoted to captain, or troop commander, leading detachments that specialized in rescue and retrieval. They began in Toronto, fighting the omnics to save as many civilians as they could from the heart of the city. Some people had barricaded themselves in their downtown condos, or were holed up on the high floors of office skyscrapers. Chase and her team helped rescue the commuters who were stuck in stranded subway train cars and those huddled, terrified, on the platforms.

It was hard, exhausting work; she lost friends in the struggle, in the underground tunnels that had collapsed, or from smoke inhalation, or facing down a squad of omnics, or in unstable buildings that crashed like dominos into the streets.

Whenever Chase thinks of them now, she shudders with dread at how close she has been, so many times, to her own end.

Other times, she reminds herself of one of their first missions, reuniting a family whose children fled when their omnic classroom assistants began attacking. Whenever she feels disheartened or grief-stricken, she recalls the faces of their parents in the camp when she and her squadron returned with both kids, shaken but safe. Their tears of relief, the look of gratitude in their eyes that even now she turns away from, still lost in her own private shame. She might not have been able to save Bonnie—who is still gravely ill in a children's hospital in Quebec, where she and her family were evacuated—but every day, Chase works to unite families and keep people safe.

And Chase has another family now, too: a squadron of twenty-four troops divided into four detachments within Canadian special forces. These small groups of soldiers are each led by their own commander: Sergeants Matthew Avery, Héloïse Camille, and Luke Harper. Chase leads the fourth detachment, which contains the squadron's specialists in medical, communications, and EOD (Explosives Ordinance Disposal), as well as their sniper. Sergeant Noah Forstall is the squad's sniper and also an expert in the employment of weapons systems including small arms, air defense systems, and antitank weaponry. Helena Dean is the Communications Sergeant, who acts as their critical link to the rest of the world while on missions. Taking point on medical is Sergeant Andre Mason. Jonathan Grayson is their EOD Sergeant; with his background in engineering, everyone likes to joke that he's just as good at building bridges as he is at blowing them apart. Because a lot of Special Forces missions involve destroying or disabling omnic technology, the CAF rely on the expertise of their EOD specialists more than they ever have before.

In the beginning, they thought it would be over soon. "When this is all over," her troops would say to one another with the silent acknowledgment that this war couldn't go on for very long. Easy to believe, in the start. At first, they had the upper hand, had more firepower than the omnics and achieved air supremacy in short order. For a moment it looked as if the Canadian army had managed to subdue the robots. Securing the cities, establishing perimeters, and quarantining evac routes was a weeks-long effort, but Chase believed it was achievable, led the one fight that ultimately succeeded in expelling the omnics from Toronto. Two weeks after the Crisis began, they were all joking about getting back to their families for Christmas.

The tide turned soon, though. At the start of the Crisis, they heard reports that the omniums—the fully automated robot-producing factories designed by Omnica Corp—had turned themselves back online. And two weeks into the battle, more omnics began to appear, replacing the numbers the CAF had defeated. These were not costumed nannies like her sister's or automated retail workers. These were militarized robots— Bastion E-54s with self-repair systems that had first been designed by human hands—units that Chase had only ever seen deployed in war zones, fresh off some assembly line, determined to kill. These units fought alongside newer horrors: OR14s with arm-mounted automatic rifles and superheated swords, or ATW-Huntsman units, spiderlike robots that crawled up the highway twenty to a man, straight from the once-defunct omnium across the American border. These new warbots have put Chase and her troops on a losing stance.

Chase knows the CAF has fought relentlessly since the onset of the Crisis, and she also knows they're losing. New responsibilities are added to her plate with each successful mission, each day her squad survives. What started as rescue and retrieval has now turned to a host of specialties. Now they also rely on her team to scout areas of active combat, report on their positions, and propose new troop formations and strategies to outwit the omnics. Every passing hour, her job gets harder. The omnics are learning from them. Predicting their moves, improving their defenses. Chase lives and breathes the war now, waking early to review fresh field data or to run drills with her detachments; after missions, she'll often fall asleep in the strategy room, considering the next day's fight.

One evening Sergeant Helena Dean, whose friendship Chase has grown to rely on, woke her up and said, "You can't fall asleep here every night." In her dream-addled state, Chase forgot where she was. Thought she was back home, in her parents' spare bedroom, waking to the smell of her mother's cooking. But then, with Helena's hand on her shoulder, everything came back to her—the Crisis, the war, everything they'd lost and what was still left to lose.

Chase touched her cheek and was surprised to find it wet. "I don't know . . ."

"It's the way we're all feeling," Helena said, her freckled heart-shaped face gentle in the moonlight. "Grief."

The grief isn't just for the people, though the thought of them weighs heavy on Chase's mind. It is something about the suddenness of the Crisis that she's never been able to come to terms with. She'll think about herself, what she was doing the week before, or the week before that—some outreach program with schoolkids who wanted to join the CAF, answering their questions in a sunlit classroom, the sound of a mower outside, the smell of cut grass and pencil shavings, the distant beat of music from the landscapers' shed. Everything was so normal then; no one had any idea of the devastation that was coming. She'll get sad randomly sometimes, at the sight of empty streets, playgrounds boarded up, swings pulled off their hinges. The unlit windows of shopping malls. Footage from around the world, a Titan smashing the copper dome of London's St.

Paul's Cathedral like the shell of an egg. Missiles just missing Shanghai's World Financial Center. The last time she saw her sister. A frightened, irrational voice in her head that asks, *What if it stays like this forever?*

And another that tells her, *If something doesn't change soon, the omnics will win.*

This mission was her idea. Two days ago, the communications specialists at CSOR managed to make contact with a detachment they'd lost a couple of weeks prior. The soldiers were part of a rescue team that had gone in to evacuate Ville-Marie, a borough of downtown Montréal that had been overrun by warbots.

They'd ended up stranded in Jour de Chance, an upscale shopping center that had made headlines a couple of years ago when its manager had refused to sign a contract that would have provided them with robotic retail assistants to replace the human employees. A decision that had seemed regressive at the time but now prescient. Like many of the buildings in Montréal's Underground City, Jour de Chance has an extensive network of underground tunnels and structures that—when the omnics began attacking downtown—had turned the shopping center into a fortress, a beacon for lingering survivors in Montréal. The refugees and, later, the rescue squadron had managed to barricade themselves in and wait for backup.

"Sounds like they've been there for weeks," one of the communications specialists explained during a briefing. Their team had made a 3D reconstruction of the buildings, the network of tunnels and subterranean shops that stretched for miles.

"I wonder how they're living," said Sergeant Noah Forstall.

"It's a miracle whatever supplies and ammunition they have even lasted this long," Chase said. "And it's a good thing the evacuation mission—"

"Who said anything about an evacuation mission?" Major Campbell asked, leaving Chase stunned. It was clear to her that they would need to evacuate the civilians and stranded troops as soon as possible before the survivors were too weak to be moved.

"You got some sort of death wish, Chase?" Campbell said, gesturing to the 3D reconstruction rotating on the large monitor screen. It was true. Chase didn't need the detailed map to understand that getting into the shopping center—considering the way that downtown Montréal was completely swarmed by omnics—would be like trying to storm a fortified castle. But Chase had made a vow to herself, after that day in the park, that as troop commander she wouldn't leave people behind— whether they were her troops or civilians.

"They're our people," Chase said, wondering how she would have felt if it had been Noah or Helena trapped in there. Wouldn't she have done anything to save them? "And they've managed to survive this long. How can it be for nothing?"

"We have to make some hard choices," Commanding Officer Fournier said.

But this was one choice Chase was not willing to make. She stayed up most of the night, examining the 3D reconstruction of the area and comparing it to old maps of the city. That was how she noticed the decommissioned utility tunnels snaking through the underground, old passages built to carry utility lines, electricity, steam, water supply pipes, and sewer pipes. Based on their aerial surveillance of omnic activity, Chase could safely conclude that the omnics didn't know about these tunnels, likely because most of them had fallen out of use decades ago. It was a happy discovery, she realized, a way in.

The next day, she presented her findings to her commanding officers and the detachment commanders. She'd worked hard to draw up a draft concept of operations, which involved infiltrating Jour de Chance via the abandoned utility tunnels.

No matter how stealthy they managed to be, the presence of the CAF was bound to draw the attention of the omnics nearby. But here the tunnels could also be turned to their advantage. Aboveground they would have been outnumbered and quickly surrounded, but underground, she hoped they would be able to funnel the omnics through the narrow corridors to better their odds.

Campbell was opposed to it, but Chase had gone over his head to pitch it to the more senior officers, who were impressed by her meticulous planning and commitment to the civilians and troops. She made a compelling case for saving what many considered to be a lost asset in the stranded detachment, and bolstered the appeal with the valuable data they could glean running a small mission in Montréal, probing the omnics for weak spots in the city's defenses.

After a short time to convene, the brass authorized the mission. But when Chase headed down the hall toward the armory,

Campbell was there to remind her: "You stuck your neck out for this mission." Then he leaned in, unblinking, threat in his tone, "If anything goes wrong, it's on you."

As with most evac runs, it doesn't take long for things to start going wrong.

The first part of their mission is a success. It takes less than an hour for Chase and her unit to make it into the shopping center's bright central atrium where the captives are gathered. Chase is overjoyed to see almost a hundred of them have survived the siege, living for months on food stores from the concession stands and delicatessens. Bundled in clothes taken from designer outlets. "Not a bad way to live," Helena whispers with a tired smirk.

Their charges are soldiers and civilians, tourists and retirees. A group of school-age children, who burst into overjoyed tears at the prospect of returning home to their families. Chase hasn't the heart to tell them that "home" has changed forever, that the people they love might already be gone, but she promises to try her best to get them out safely.

"We didn't know how long we'd last," says one of the soldiers. "A couple more days, maybe. We've been running low on everything. Water, ammo . . . It's a miracle you found us." Although he's bundled up in clothes salvaged from the closed stores, he wears a white camo hood, the same as her own, that identifies him as a member of the special forces.

"I'd like to hope someone would do the same for me," Chase tells him.

As her detachment helps to rearm the soldiers, one of the combat supporters makes contact over the comms. "Chase, we're detecting signs of increased omnic activity in your area."

"Copy that." This is what Chase expected. "Send me the locations."

"It looks like they've completely blocked off the utility tunnels you came in by."

"So we'll have to leave a different way." Chase also planned for this. She divides the gathered people among her detachments and instructs two of them to leave via separate exits through the subterranean network of shops, offices, entertainment venues, and metro stations in the heart of downtown. Chase knows there are more than 120 exterior access points that can act as escape routes, but these are also areas the omnics may infiltrate.

"Time is of the essence," she reminds them. "In ten minutes we'll have an evacuation team ready to take everyone to safety. But our window to board is small—they can't linger long."

She can tell there is some nervousness among all the soldiers about the change of plan. It's been only minutes, but by now the omnics have likely mapped all the utility tunnels and are flooding toward their position. They will know the Underground City well, which means that her people could be walking into an ambush—with civilians in tow.

Chase hopes that leaving via separate exits means at least some of them will make it out of Jour de Chance alive. But as her detachment members and leaders rush underground, she can't help but imagine a darker outcome—the sound of all their voices on the comms, distant screams, the crackle and hiss of her earpiece, and then—silence.

Chase runs now, leading a party of twenty people—four of her detachment members, along with the stranded soldiers and the civilian children—through an unopened extension of the Underground City. In some places it's nearly new, posh shops with ghostly mannequins striking poses in darkened windows. In others, she can tell where construction work was abandoned before it could be completed. Exposed light fixtures hang from the ceiling, uninsulated wires curling behind pristine plastic cones.

"I think we took this turn already," Noah says. Chase has the sinking feeling that he's right and they could be lost. As soon as they came down into the tunnel she lost communication with combat support—likely their enemy jamming the signal. Although Chase thought she'd memorized these passages, everything seems different now, down here in the half light, with most of the walls crumbling.

"I think it's that way," says Helena, pointing. "Three hundred meters, maybe, to the Place des Arts. We took a left back there when we should have gone right."

With most of the overhead lights blown to shattered glass, they're relying on their infrared-vision goggles, though Chase's cybernetic eyes mean she doesn't need to wear them. So far, she can't see any sign of an exit, but when they take the next right Chase catches a glimpse of a figure behind a chipboard wall. Omnics have different heat signatures from humans. Their bodies are cool as steel, so nothing but the power core in their chest lights up in the blackness.

Chase barely has the time to cry out a warning before it's racing for her.

It's an OR14. These warbots have become front-line combatants since the Crisis. Chase has disabled dozens of these since the war began. They look more alien than the humanoid omnics she's spent most of the last months clearing from the streets. This one has a matte-gray titanium frame covered by its polished orange chest plating and yellow visual sensors that glow like a jackal's eyes in the darkness. It's twice the size of a human, so big it needs to crouch in the low-ceilinged tunnels. Difficult to look at one, in this place, without fear creeping up her spine.

Chase lifts her rail gun and lets out a rapid burst of fire. She loves the weapon; this particular prototype was only recently built by the CAF's research and development division. It uses electromagnetic force to launch high-velocity projectiles that can pierce almost anything. (This prototype wasn't put into circulation, as the recoil was deemed too strong for the average soldier to aim accurately. Not her, though.)

Chase manages to land a critical hit on the OR14. It falls to its knees, spraying hydraulic fluid.

The children behind her scream, and Helena, who has taken the rear, works quickly to calm them. "We need to keep moving," Chase says. She thinks she can hear the sound of more warbots marching up the tunnel toward them, the vibration of their heavy bodies in the ground, the hiss of hydraulics as they move.

As they run past more closed shops and restaurants, Chase sees the shadow of something behind the glass.

She doesn't duck in time to miss it—an explosion of bullets from a fusion driver. Glass shards are everywhere, and at first, Chase only understands that she's been hit because the side of her body slams against the opposite wall. The impact sends sparks flying in her head, and she hears a sound in her skull like something delicate snapping. Her eye, she thinks.

Then pain, her peripheral nerves are on fire. She peels herself off the splintered chipboard to find that her left leg is leaking hydraulic fluid.

"Chase!" Helena's voice, as more bullets rend the air.

The civilians take cover as Luca and Avery fire enough projectiles at the OR14 to disarm it. It lances at Luca with its superheated metal sword. He ducks out of the way in time to watch it burn a hole into the wall.

More omnics advance toward them from three directions: in front, behind, and via the unlit passage perpendicular to them. With a sinking feeling in her stomach, Chase realizes that her plan has backfired horribly. Instead of funneling the enemy, the route has allowed the warbots to make a pincer movement on Chase and her detachments.

They take a defensive stance around the civilians they're escorting to safety, and the assault begins. Up through the tunnel Chase sees the glowing eyes of more OR14s, their superheated swords cutting a path through the darkness. The constricted space limits how fast the robots can travel, but, looking at the cracks in the walls, the bricks flaying from the ceiling as they absorb some of the damage from the omnic's projectiles, Chase is beginning to worry that the tunnel may collapse on them.

With the lens of one eye broken, it's much harder for her to take accurate aim at the enemy, but Chase tries her best, rapid-firing at the oncoming OR14s and landing enough hits by sheer luck to fell them.

Chase orders her troops to lay down suppressing fire at the units nearest them, then turns to Noah, the most reliable sharpshooter on the team, and directs him to fire at the more distant line of OR14s.

"Helena," she shouts, "are comms still down? We can't hold them off for very long here. We need to relay an SOS back to base."

"I'll try," she says, sounding uncertain.

Under the clatter of gunfire she listens for the sound of bullets piercing titanium, the hiss of ruptured limbs and sputtering electronics. One OR14 drops to the floor a couple of meters from Chase, sparks crackling from its chest, into a spreading puddle of hydraulic fluid. The sight is frightening. If they don't manage to make it out soon, they could all be electrocuted or burned alive down here.

Avery has a few grenades in his arsenal and asks Chase for permission to use them. With the walls trembling and plaster crashing from the ceiling, it seems like a desperate move.

"Hold off for the moment," Chase says.

"For what?" he says quietly, a hollow look in his eyes. She can see the fear there, that they're all going to die down here.

"If you detonate that thing, the walls will collapse, and this fight will be over," she tells him.

"It's just a matter of time before—" He doesn't want to say it, but the omnics are closing in. Chase's fingers on her weapon are cold with dread. Has she led her troops—and children and civilians—to their deaths?

"Maybe we can take cover in one of the shops?" Helena suggests. Chase eyes the bullet-riddled mannequins in the shattered window of an outerwear store. As she does, a piece of tile comes loose from the ceiling and just misses her.

We're not going to make it, Chase thinks. *Even if we manage to hold the robots off, how long until this tunnel collapses on us?*

Chase's mind races through several desperate plans. *Sacrifice,* she thinks now. She and her detachment could go on the offensive and draw omnic fire to help the civilians escape. Have Grayson use the grenades to collapse the tunnel, seal off the omnics' exit so the survivors can't be pursued.

Chase turns to the tunnel on her left, where a solid phalanx of warbots glitters menacingly as they approach, ready to take aim and shower their enemy with bullets. She takes in a breath to give the order.

"What's that sound?" Master Corporal Luca asks. A storm of gunfire on the other side of the tunnel. Chase instructs the civilians and soldiers to take cover as the OR14s fall like dominoes. They are destroyed almost all at once, and Chase watches as the lights of their sensors grow dim. Their salvation.

When she switches her vision to infrared, she can see a dozen figures on the other side of the tunnel, their bodies like torches in the blackness. More of her soldiers? Another detachment from CSOR come to rescue them? They're wearing blue uniforms she doesn't recognize, though.

"State your rank!" Chase shouts.

There are about thirty of them, the heels of their boots beating a steady march through the dark tunnel. Chase can see the outline of their captain, a tall blond man who takes the last omnic out with a well-aimed shot of his rifle. She squints at the glow of his scanner in the gloom, a speck of light glinting off his gun.

"Captain Jack Morrison," he says.

The man behind him with the braided beard shouts in a thick accent, "Chief Engineer Torbjörn Lindholm!"

"Who are you with?" Chase calls now.

She feels as if she could have dreamed them. This fleet of soldiers dressed in blue, a white-and-orange logo on their chests. They're not from the CAF.

"We're Overwatch."

2

LAURENTIDES

"They called us in when the combat supporters lost contact with your detachment," the captain explains as their combined troops rush past them toward the cleared exit.

Overwatch. She's heard of them. Rumors, mostly, and some grumbling from higher up the chain of command. An international task force focused on ending the Crisis. Early on, they began recruiting soldiers from militaries around the world—calling for volunteers and taking some of the CAF's best troops. Tales of their strike team, though, seem to possess an almost mythic quality. The Overwatch strike team are a small elite force, bringing together fighters from across the globe: a Crusader from Germany, Egypt's best sniper, and a few who were said to be almost superhuman in their abilities.

Captain Jack Morrison smiles at her now, even as the tunnel

crumbles around them. "Looks like we arrived just in time."

Chase hefts her rifle. "Earlier would have been great too."

As the last of their troops file past, Chase and Jack begin to follow. She can see light up ahead, the exit—they're almost there. Chase is pleased to see her team and Overwatch fall into a similar rhythm as they race to get the civilians out. They rush in the darkness over the bullet-riddled bodies of omnics.

Chase hears the sound of a rumble overhead, the other ground forces engaging the omnics in a fight aboveground. The sound of an explosion topside sends vibrations through the tunnel, the ceiling pelting them with dust and plaster. Chase ducks in time to miss a brick that shakes loose from the ceiling and crashes onto the floor with enough force to crack the head of one of the felled omnics.

A scream up ahead makes her pick up her pace, though. One of the captive soldiers falls to his knees with a shout of pain. "Were you hit?" Chase asks.

"My leg," he howls through a clenched jaw, his face red with pain.

Even as he does, though, there is another explosion above. The rattle causes several intact light bulbs to blow out, raining glass splinters across the ground and in Chase's hair. She ducks instinctively to shield the man.

"I can't move," he shouts. "Go on without me."

"No!" Chase looks up ahead. They need to run. Even this pause has opened a gap of a few meters between the two of them, Jack, and the rest of the team. If they don't run now, they might not make it out.

The soldier sees it too. "Go!" he says. "I'll only slow you down."

"I'm not leaving until everyone is out." Chase struggles to take in the situation quickly. He won't be able to walk; she feels a little queasy looking at the way his boot is twisted.

"It's going to be okay." Chase stoops down and takes his arm, pulling it up over her shoulder. She counts to three, and with a heave, he's up off the floor, leaning most of his weight on her. "We'll get you help soon."

It's hard for them to walk together. In order to hold on to him, Chase needs to abandon one of her weapons in the tunnel. She thinks about picking him up, but even bearing half his weight, she feels the extent of her injuries more acutely. Every step on her right leg causes a lightning bolt of pain to shoot up to her thigh. Although Chase trudges through it, it's slow going. She worries about her leg buckling and causing them both to topple over. A couple of times Chase pulls him in close to dodge falling bricks or bits of scorched plasterboard, and he cries out in pain, accidentally putting weight on his injured ankle. As they hurry, Chase thinks about miners racing from a shaft before an explosion. It's difficult to see for the smoke and dust, or to hear over the sound of gunfire echoing through the once-polished tunnels.

It's a relief when her feet find the metal grates of an immobile escalator. She and the soldier hobble up it and to the Place des Arts, where light cascades in. The afternoon sun makes disorienting prisms in Chase's shattered lens, and she closes one eye. The hammer and rattle of gunfire are still ringing in her ears. Aboveground is its own battlefield. Omnics are closing in from all directions, but the CAF have managed to hold them off just long enough to help civilians and soldiers into the large stratoscopters grounded on the public square.

Her detachment and the civilians they escorted have all crawled up to safety, coughing and sputtering, and now they are aboveground, people running in all directions. Another squadron of the Overwatch team has remained above to support the CAF in battle. Hers is the last detachment to emerge from the Underground City. And as soon as they do, combat supporters meet the civilians—who have stumbled blinking in the sunlight, bewildered as newborn lambs—to direct them to the evac.

"Thank you," the soldier by her side says softly to Chase as he's ushered away by the medical team.

Chase boards the stratoscopter with the rest of her detachments, and as they take off, the sound of the fray grows quieter.

"We made it," Helena says. She's sitting next to Chase and squeezes her hand happily when the stratoscopter accelerates.

"Just," Chase exhales, looking around at her team, counting the faces; Helena and Noah, Jake and Mason, Luca, Harper, Avery . . .

There's a familiar plunge in her stomach as they rise into the air. She squeezes her eyes shut against the swoop of nausea. Under the rumble of the engine, she hears a sound like rainfall in the forest or galloping hooves. When Chase opens her eyes again, she realizes that everyone is clapping. They're clapping for her.

"Captain Vivian Chase advocated for this mission," comes the voice of Commanding Officer Fournier over the comms. "One hundred and seven civilians saved, besides our stranded squad. I think I'd call that a success."

Chase flushes a little at the attention.

"But," says Major Campbell, "let's not forget the efforts of the Overwatch strike team. Today would have turned out differently if we hadn't requested Overwatch reroute to your location and provide support."

Chase eyes them now. By accident, or habit, her team are all strapped in on one side of the cabin, and the strike team, in their blue uniforms, are on the other. Overwatch. Their name echoes now among her soldiers. Most of them have barely heard of the group, though. Chase herself has only heard their name in awed whispers or in terse commentary from above. Slightly surreal to find herself in their presence now.

Captain Jack Morrison sits opposite. If she looks at him through her broken eye, his face is rendered a dozen times as if in a kaleidoscope. Error codes are beginning to flash up before her, telling her something is wrong with the machinery in her head. Where her peripheral nerves remain, she can feel the distant throb of pain and swelling in her flesh. Chase clenches a fist through it as he says, "I've heard a lot about you, Captain Chase."

She's heard almost nothing about him and isn't completely certain what Overwatch is doing here, though she's certainly grateful they came. At the same time, she's sure she'll get an earful in the mission debrief back at base for needing the help.

To his left is a short but burly blond man who introduced

himself as Torbjörn Lindholm. He looks striking in his armor, with a long braided beard and heavy brow. Chase knows that he is one of the greatest weaponsmiths and engineers alive. He's gained some notoriety for designing weapons that have been deployed in wars around the world, but Chase has heard him on the news speaking disparagingly about the scientists at Omnica Corp. She knows that Torbjörn believes their reckless ambition caused the Crisis, and she can't help but agree.

"I hope you weren't injured too badly," comes a voice from a couple of seats down. It's from a woman with hazel eyes and thick jet hair plaited beneath an oversize helmet. She looks tiny and out of place among the other soldiers.

"Nothing I can't handle," Chase lies. In truth, she's beginning to feel a little panicked about the injury to her lens, though she tries not to let her mind spin out into catastrophic thinking. What if the base's medic can't fix it, and she is forced on medical leave?

"I'm happy to take a look at your lens if you need it."

Chase recoils, thinking, *How does she know?*

"Sorry?" Chase says, and the woman points to her own darkly lashed eye.

"I can tell from the glint coming off it. Refraction. Shattered during the mission? Those TFW12 lenses have a tendency to do that on impact. Bit of a design flaw."

"I'm fine," Chase insists through gritted teeth. She can feel the blood rising at the back of her neck. She hates to talk about her cybernetics in public. The questions exhaust her. Sometimes she just wants to fit in with the rest of her troops without needing to explain the ways that her body is different.

"I can fix it," the woman offers brightly.

"What are you, a doctor?"

The stratoscopter shudders a little, and the seat belt jolts against Chase's bruised shoulder in a way that makes her wince.

"This is our newest recruit, Dr. Mina Liao," Jack says.

"Newest *trial* recruit," Torbjörn corrects.

"Oh," Chase says softly. "Sorry, I didn't realize . . ."

"It's okay," Dr. Liao says. "Technically, I'm not cleared for field operations. They rerouted us to your position midflight, so I'm just—"

Torbjörn huffs. "Long story short, she's not supposed to be here."

Dr. Liao was briefly a media sensation, a child prodigy, the youngest roboticist at Omnica Corp. On television, she talked with passion about artificial intelligence and the untapped potential of omnics. In the preceding years, Omnica had grown in status from a scrappy start-up to a massive disrupter on the world stage. Liao joined at a moment when Omnica Corp had seemingly nowhere else to go with its omnics—they asked her to improve on something that many thought couldn't be improved. But when she bent her efforts toward creating the next generation of adaptive AI, the doctor and her team succeeded beyond anyone's wildest expectations. They were thrust further into the spotlight when their prototype, Aurora, was declared sentient. Dr. Liao campaigned to give Aurora personhood, and she eventually won.

Although no one knows for certain what caused the Omnic Crisis—not even Omnica Corp's former employees—as far as

Chase is concerned, their present situation is entirely the fault of their scientists. It was they who plowed heedlessly toward the "future," ensured there was an omnic in every home. And it's their fully automated, self-sustaining factories—the omniums—that are churning out warbots every hour. When she looks at the faces of people like Dr. Liao, she sees Bonnie in the field hospital, Valentine's despair, those terrified civilians they just rescued, and the millions more who died crying out for help.

"You're in Overwatch?" Chase has a hard time keeping the incredulity from her voice. There is a ripple of tension in the cabin, then. Soldiers all around shift uncomfortably. So, Chase thinks, she's not the only one who's noticed the conflict; someone who helped create these robots is working now to fight and defeat them.

"Yes," Jack says, a flash of defiance in his blue eyes. "Dr. Liao is going to be leading counter-omnic research for our strike team. And we are honored to have her."

Dr. Liao bows her head, her cheeks red.

Torbjörn looks away.

Chase doesn't say anything else, nor does anyone, for a while.

From the porthole, the streets of downtown Montréal unfurl. So different from the city Chase remembers: half the landmarks have collapsed. Just below she sees a university, its neoclassical buildings abandoned now, windows blown in, shattered spires and smashed brick. From above, she can clearly see the extent of the invasion. Bastion tanks fill the streets, the parks, the malls; arcades and museums are packed with OR14s. Farther uptown, the air force continues their campaign of air strikes and bombings in the unpopulated areas where there is still heavy omnic activity. Everything is covered with a patina of smoke and dust.

It's always dizzying to see her world so changed. The RCAF may be making headway in the air, but it's impossible to match the omnics for sheer firepower and numbers. For every one of their soldiers, it seems there are almost a dozen omnics. And more pouring out of the Detroit omnium every single day. The enemy, as Chase has come to consider them.

And while her troops and comrades might win a battle or deplete their forces bit by bit, the omnics learn from them, can adapt almost instantaneously. They find ways to leverage any weakness, and they come back reinforced, more lethal. Chase feels as if she is running out of clever plans to outwit them.

The war reminds her of the game her grandfather, a retired admiral, invented when she was younger. In order to occupy her time during long hospital stays, he took an old chess set and devised a new game he called Shah Matt: "The King Is Dead." He retained the chess board and its one hundred squares, but replaced knights with tanks, the bishop with an inventor, and added a prime minister alongside the king. There was a wildcard ability to make simultaneous moves, or to "overwhelm" the enemy so they couldn't move at all. Chase loved it, almost as much as the time they spent together, their shadows thrown across the board. She cherished the hours of his careful attention, his wisdom. She even loved the time in between visits when she would lie in bed and devise elaborate, complicated campaigns to confound and delight him.

She was in the middle of plotting one on the night he died.

"I was going to win this time" were the first words out of her mouth when her father told her. Really, Chase wanted to express that she would miss his mind, his steady mentorship, his company. His love.

After her grandfather's death, her family inherited his omnic caretaker, the unit issued by the VAC in his old age. The omnic became her new—albeit colder—hospital companion, and she taught the machine to play Shah Matt with her. But playing against the omnic felt completely different. It learned so fast. Soon, Chase was no match for the machine's razor-edged intelligence and cool precision. It could anticipate her moves so accurately that they often nudged their pieces to opposite squares at the exact same time.

These battles they are fighting now against the omnics feel much the same. Her troops are exhausted and stretched too thin. Today's victory has energized them for a little while, but tomorrow it will be back into the old fight. Back to trying to conceive of wilder ways to defeat the enemy. And the day after that?

Chase tries to shake the anxiety away, shake the cold fingers of dread that have been tightening on her shoulders. She's scared they will lose—and terrified of what the world will be like if they do.

The base is almost invisible against the mountains, especially after a fresh snowfall. Once they land, the detachments gather in the strategy room for the after-action report. The room is on the top floor of the base, with windows on one side that reveal a bright view of the snowy mountainside. The opposite wall is covered in monitor screens and displays, graphs and projections, maps and schematics. A couple that always draw Chase's attention are the large aerial displays of major cities with expanding red zones that indicate current omnic activity.

The commanding officers are already seated at the laminated wood table. The room smells of instant coffee.

"As you know," says Commanding Officer Fournier, her face backlit blue by the screen behind her, "the enemy's main point of entry is here, where the Detroit omnium feeds new units and supplies directly into the country." The omnium is a little red circle on the map just at the border. Chase has never seen an omnium in person, but she imagines it must be like a wasp's nest, buzzing with ceaseless activity. Cold, silent robots being assembled on factory lines, their minds lit up with a singular awful purpose.

"We have requested and received Overwatch support to help us permanently clear the omnics out of the southern cities, down to Toronto, where we will establish a permanent perimeter our infantry can enforce."

Sounds ambitious, Chase thinks. She knows that Overwatch is an international team with plenty of resources, but she's seen what they are up against. Most of the CAF's actions have been focused on protecting Quebec. CSOR has been running guerrilla missions in the south with a skeleton crew—mostly last ditch efforts to save civilians or secure needed resources.

"We can't match the omnic numbers, but we have managed

to achieve air supremacy, since the omnics have been focused on the ground invasion. It's time we press that advantage. And now the United Nations has sent us all the resources of Overwatch, including their chief engineer, Torbjörn Lindholm, and their research director, Dr. Mina Liao. Together, they have cooperated on a cutting-edge defense system, which includes a fleet of devices called 'herons.'" With a hand gesture, the device appears on the screen. It does look like a bird, a kind of drone with a long neck and antennae that hang down.

Liao stands then, the projection casting her features in electric blue. "The herons," she explains, "are invisible to omnics."

"How can you be sure?" asks EOD Sergeant Grayson.

Liao smiles, though she looks a little annoyed by the interruption. "They exploit the omnics' sensor systems in a way that allows the herons to fly long distances undetected, which makes them excellent at intelligence gathering. They can fly over a perimeter and scan the ground for signs of omnic movement. Once omnic activity is detected, they send a warning back to base, which can then deploy and direct Torbjörn's—"

Torbjörn gets loudly to his feet. "These new turrets can move, fire fast, and they pack an even bigger punch than what I made back home. Once deployed, they'll turn any tin can within range to scrap."

"We're calling it a siege," Liao adds.

"*The Siege*," Torbjörn corrects without looking at her.

"The collective noun for herons," she continues brightly. "Fascinating birds. Just like our system, when hunting their prey they stay completely still. They watch and wait and then—"

"Bang!" Torbjörn slams his fist on the table so hard it sends coffee mugs clattering, and everyone jumps. "Strategically placed," he goes on, his voice booming in the startled silence, "the Siege system will give you the upper hand against the omnics."

After they both sit down, there is a smattering of nervous whispers. Finally, Chase requests permission to speak. "This sounds great," she begins, "but my unit has just spent the better part of three months trying to defeat the omnics, and—"

"And your hard work and hard-won victories are an essential part of this new mission, Captain," Commanding Officer Fournier cuts in. She points to the map again, where locations in Ottawa and Montréal are now lit green.

"We've identified key points of combat where we believe the Siege is most capable of building on your already impressive progress. We will need you, Captain Morrison, and your combined troops to defend Torbjörn and his engineers, to hold off the omnic attack long enough for the team to install the Siege units and initiate the program."

"We all know the exacting cost of urban warfare," Campbell says. "Defender always has the advantage. Overwatch's technology will be embedded in the cities themselves, leveling the playing field when it comes to both intelligence and firepower."

Helena turns to Chase. "The herons alone will give us enough data for you to have a field day."

"Based on your success thus far," Fournier continues, "it's been agreed that Captain Chase will run CSOR's tactical support for Overwatch's mission, leading the partnership from the Canadian side."

"Thank you," Chase says. The pain from her injuries is making it hard to focus. Her head feels as if it's twisted in with razor wire and her leg is gripped in a vise.

Jack stands and offers the room a winning smile, his hair silvered in the light through the window. "It's an honor to work with you," he tells them, "and I'm confident that our combined efforts will bring us another step closer to victory for Canada, and all of humanity."

A couple of people applaud at this, or cheer their agreement. Chase doesn't, though.

She admires the plan, but she's not convinced that even with Overwatch's combined firepower they will be able to hold off the omnics long enough to install the Siege. Especially given the extensive installation needs in areas of heavy activity pinpointed on the map.

More than anything, Chase is not convinced by Jack's hope. She's been fighting for so long and lost so much that hope, for her, feels almost impossible to come by.

"Only a couple more minutes," comes Liao's disembodied voice over the speaker. Chase keeps as still as she can in the scanner. She's used to the sound of it, the mechanical whirr and hum. When she was younger, she'd amuse herself by imagining little elves inside the monitor, painting a picture of her bones and tendons with lightning-quick speed.

"All done," Liao says at the moment the speaker pings and

the doors slide open. Outside, she's perched on a chair by the monitor. She motions for Chase to sit on the gurney, but Chase would rather stand.

At the base's infirmary, the doctor on call was able to fix the damage that her leg sustained in the Underground City, but one look at her eye and he told her he didn't have the expertise to replace the shattered lens. "I specialize in wetware," he said, shaking his head, "not hardware." In his opinion, Chase was lucky Liao was here to help. Chase grudgingly agreed.

"Whatever hit you must have hurt," Liao says now, staring at the monitor where a 3D reconstruction of her eye is rendered. Liao manipulates the image on her plexi data pad, leaning forward. She glances quizzically up at her patient.

"I have a high pain tolerance," Chase says.

"It would seem so . . . ," the doctor says with a low whistle. A hand motion reveals the display of the rest of Chase's body. "Such extensive cybernetics at such a young age. How old were you?"

"Thirteen. For the first couple of operations. The big ones. But more modifications as I grew."

"Wow. I've never seen anything like this. And this too . . ." Liao zooms in on Chase's heart. It's a device the size of a navel orange, made of transparent silicone and titanium valves and spurs. Instead of pumping, it has a spinning metal disc inside that continuously pushes her blood through its chambers. It's part of the reason her pulse can be difficult to detect.

Chase feels uneasy, though, watching the doctor marvel at her as if she's a cadaver prone in front of a classroom of medical students.

"This configuration of your heart and lungs . . ." Liao squints at the display. "It must provide a decent metabolic advantage."

It's true, Chase can run faster and for longer than unaugmented humans, and she had little trouble adjusting to the higher altitudes at the mountain base.

"I could probably win a gold medal for sprinting," Chase jokes, but then dismisses the thought. "Though I probably wouldn't be allowed to compete in any games."

Swiping away a notification on her data pad, Liao muses playfully, "I suppose it would depend on their cyborg policy. Some competitions do—" But she senses her mistake immediately and says, "Oh—forgive me, I wasn't thinking."

Chase hates that word: *cyborg*. It brings back echoes of high school, the way the other students in her school shrank away from her or spoke about her in whispers. Some of them even tried to catch a glimpse of her cybernetic legs during gym class.

"They used to call me—" She interrupts herself. "Never mind." She doesn't owe Liao any of her life story.

"So . . ." Liao pivots the conversation by switching the display on the monitor. "The bad news is that they don't make eyes like yours anymore. Those lenses especially."

Chase tries to hide her disappointment—getting used to new hardware takes time she doesn't have, particularly given her latest directive.

"But we have newer, better models," Liao continues. "I can do the procedure now to replace them and install the necessary software update to make them compatible. I will of course have to replace both of them so that they match. My expertise is obviously in omnics, but this is a procedure I've read a lot about."

"That's reassuring to hear," Chase says dryly. It irks her to be lumped in with robots—and, if she's being honest, with Liao in general, given her role in the Crisis.

"There are actually quite a few upgrades I could make to your cybernetics with your consent. This one will definitely improve your eyesight, but while you're under, I can make some alterations to the operating system that runs your spine and nerves. It would vastly improve your reflexes, make you stronger and much faster—"

"Let's just fix the issue at hand," Chase says. She doesn't want this to take any longer than it has to.

Chase has always hated being put to sleep. She still remembers the way her father's eyes glistened the first time a doctor wheeled her into the OR. She always believed he was the most stoic man in the world—a soldier, quiet and steadfast. The sight of tears in his eyes frightened her even before the procedure began. Almost twenty years later, she was still unnerved by the feeling of the cannula in her hand, or the sudden pressure as the anesthesiologist pressed the syringe and shunted milky liquid into her veins. She would always try to cling on. But her consciousness became a helium balloon quickly untethering from the inside of her skull. Whatever thought she fell asleep with—*We are such stuff as dreams are made on, and our little life is rounded with a sleep*—would echo at the edge of her awareness on the other side.

Chase opens her eyes now, feeling as if no time has passed. Though, disconcertingly, it always has. Sometimes it's hours; this time it's forty minutes.

"Careful." Liao's voice.

Chase's hands had flown immediately to her eyes, to the dressings on them.

"Slowly."

When she pulls the dressings off, she is sun blind, the strip lights above her head bleaching her vision seafoam green. Her first thought is that it didn't work. Panic, fury—but then, when Liao's face comes into view, it's with a startling clarity. Has she always looked this way? The pores on her nose might as well be craters on the moon. The dark striations in her hazel irises have a texture as fine as grains of sand.

"Can you stand?"

Chase gets steadily to her feet. The dregs of the sedation feel as if they are sticking to her veins like tar. She rubs her eyes and looks around. Colors seem more vivid than before, as if the world is fluorescing under some filter. Outside the window, the low-hanging clouds, the trees, and the lake are all rendered in glorious detail.

"I'd like to perform a few routine checks to be sure everything is working as it should," Liao says. It takes about a quarter of an hour to run through the short-range tests and make adjustments, and by then the sun has set. Chase gravitates toward the window, shocked at the way her new eyes can pick out the constellations.

"Shall we go for a walk?" Liao suggests. "You can try out some of the long-range features."

The air outside is bracing. The snow has stopped, but clouds are wheeling fast, the wind blowing her eyes into slits.

Frost-covered pine needles crunch underfoot as they step out, toward the chain-link perimeter of the base. Behind the earth's atmosphere, the stars flicker like birthday candles. They've never looked so clear to Chase before.

"It should be fairly intuitive to you," Liao says. "The interface is similar to your old eyes."

Chase blinks and glances around, searching through the menus that flash before her. One feature links her eyes up with satellite footage, giving her a map of the local area. When she asks Liao about it, she explains that it can connect her eyes up with CSOR's intelligence network as well, giving her a detailed real-time view of the battle and where her troops are in relation to the enemy. Chase is thrilled and can't wait to practice using it in a combat scenario tomorrow morning in training.

Another feature offers longer-range infrared vision—she can see bodies in the mess hall, like pillars of lava, on the other side of the door. Far away, she can see the engine of a truck, the driver like a flame inside.

At the edge of the lake, she can make out two figures. A loping giant she recognizes and an elegant one. *Noah and Helena,* she thinks with a gossipy thrill. On another night walk together. Holding hands away from the prying eyes of the unit.

"What is it?" Liao asks at her smile.

"There's an owl in that tree over there," Chase says. She can see its hot body against the snowy branches.

"I know." Liao laughs. "I can hear it."

They walk for a little while in silence, their breath misting on the air. Chase is surprised by how delighted she is with her new eyes. It's as if the world is suddenly beautiful, or some scales have fallen away and she alone can discern how lovely it has always been. For the first time in her life, she feels a glimmer of pity for Liao, for Valentine, for her old self with her old eyes. Anyone who can't gaze at the tip of their finger and marvel at the exquisite morphology of a snowflake. Or the veins on fallen leaves latticed with crystals of frost. The fissures in the rocks of these mountains, Precambrian, she has heard, more than 514 million years old, some of the oldest in the world, rising up to meet the soles of her cybernetic feet.

It ends up being a short walk, halfway around the base. By the time they reach the armory, Liao's cheeks are windblown and her lips are chapped from the cold.

"Let's have a look in on their progress, shall we?" Liao says, but from the way she is rubbing her hands, Chase knows she just wants a reason to get out of the chill.

Chase has only been in the armory a couple of times before. It's a huge space, the size of an airplane hangar, with stationary drones, missiles and rocket launchers, tanks and rifles. Chase and the doctor enter via a metal walkway that allows them a view of the expansive place, where the newly deployed engineers from Overwatch are working at putting finishing touches on drones. Others lean over tablet computers, examining models of weapons or lines of dense code. About a dozen technicians are still unpacking everything that Overwatch arrived with that morning, machinery on pallets or in boxes, piling it up on industrial shelving.

Somewhere among them, Chase assumes, are the components of the Siege system they are hoping to deploy in Ottawa. But among the tangle of wires and weapons and Overwatch-branded boxes, she's not certain what she's looking at. She's cautiously excited to see the invention in action, despite her misgivings. She's hoping that the weapon will give them that edge over the omnics they so desperately need.

Torbjörn and two engineers stand on the opposite mezzanine, conducting a heated discussion in front of a chalkboard. The scene reminds Chase of her university statistics class. Torbjörn's hectic scrawl and the serious-looking engineers frowning at it from under their hard hats.

"He's so old-fashioned," Liao says to Chase under her breath. "He might as well use papyrus."

"I heard that," Torbjörn says, "and it behooves me to remind you that you can't hack chalk. And there's a lot to recommend papyrus, since writings have survived five thousand years. What do you think will become of your hard drives in another hundred years?"

"Torbjörn," says the white-haired woman in a hard hat standing next to him, "I'm sure we're all a fan of anything we can send around the globe at the speed of light, through optical fibers in a series of ones and zeros."

Liao tries to hide a chuckle, then she steps closer to the chalkboard. "Is this the initiation sequence?"

"For the turrets," he says. "Professor Karlsson believes she's found a solution to a bug."

The white-haired woman nods.

Liao studies the equations on the board for a moment and smiles.

"This is great work. I've actually been thinking about this too," Liao says, opening her hand for Torbjörn's chalk. "I have a suggestion that utilizes a little more redundancy."

Torbjörn tightens his fist on the chalk.

"With all due respect, Doctor, we have this in hand. And when we were asked to collaborate on this project, our agreement was that your domain would be the air and I would be left to handle the land. Herons, turrets."

Torbjörn turns back toward Karlsson and continues their conversation.

Liao and Chase head, in silence, back to the lab. Liao looks visibly deflated. Chase can see the annoyance in her face as they walk, and she feels a little sorry for her.

"What happened back there, I know what that feels like," Chase says. "I've lost track of how many times my commanding officers dismissed my ideas, and every time I have to watch the mission suffer for it. I try to remind myself that, for some people, it's more about propping up their ego than about what's best for the objective."

"I appreciate you trying to comfort me," Liao says. "But it's not the same . . . Unfortunately, I know what this is really about."

As they circle the entrance, the Canadian flag cracks violently in the wind. A security drone lights them both in red and blue before whizzing off. Chase kicks at a hardy tuft of grass peering through the snow, waiting for Liao to continue.

"They blame me for the Crisis."

"You think so?" Chase says, struggling to avert her gaze for fear of giving herself away.

"At Omnica, I knew the costs of creating Aurora—pushing those boundaries. I wanted to make the world a better place, and that science felt right. But I had many critics. Torbjörn called my work out specifically during my tenure there. He said the breakthroughs my team were making would have unforeseen consequences. After the Crisis broke out—well, let's just say he and many others thought he was very... right. At this point, I'm not sure how to gain his trust."

"But," Chase says, judging from what she saw earlier in the stratoscopter, "Jack clearly believes in you."

"And he's put his neck on the line for it," Liao adds, her voice tight. "I've heard from Strike Commander Reyes and Undersecretary Adawe that this mission is my chance to prove my worth . . . or I'm off the team."

"Well," Chase says, shaking away the flutter of guilt in her gut, "sometimes trust takes time."

"Time is one of the many things we *don't* have," Liao counters.

Chase scrunches her chilly fingers into a fist. Cold doesn't bother her so much anymore, or heat. Her cybernetic limbs can withstand a far greater range of temperatures than flesh and blood can, and pain is duller to her now—with half of her pain receptors gone. But in this weather she can still feel some stiffness in her hydraulic joints. Her tendons are slower to obey.

"Some people have been saying that the Crisis could have been predicted," Chase says. "To me, it feels as if humanity was blindsided, but you were there when it all started going sideways, pushing the limits of the technology . . ." It's hard to articulate without sounding more accusatory than Chase wants to. "Could you have guessed that this would happen?"

"Of course we could!" Liao says. "Robot apocalypse is a favorite fodder of science fiction. But it's mostly that: fiction. Those who truly know the science, who know exactly how we created the omnics, know that this destruction could never have happened as a result of our work. We were cautious when we needed to be—we coded enough fail-safes to make this kind of thing impossible."

"Clearly not 'enough,' though," Chase says. "Do you have any regrets? Aren't there some things that you would do differently, if you could?"

"Everyone does, Captain." Liao's eyes are glittering now, dark jewels in the night. "I think about my work for Omnica all the time." There is a note of almost maternal tenderness in the doctor's voice that Chase finds unsettling.

"But what about," she begins, "all the people *suffering* because of the work Omnica did?"

"Obviously, I'm heartbroken about the Crisis," Liao says. "But as I've been trying to tell people, scientists aren't prophets. We can't know for sure all the consequences of everything that we do. Do you think the people who invented glitter were thinking about microplastics poisoning the ocean? Or how the internet would threaten democracy?"

"Maybe it's their job to," Chase says.

"People want me to apologize for my work, but some of it was *good work*. The precise mechanics of your legs, the sensors in your eyes, were designed by Omnica Corp. Omnics cared for children and the elderly and the sick—did the jobs that we'd previously paid low wages for. They lifted a generation out of poverty, saved countless lives . . . up until a few months ago. And we still don't know why that changed."

Liao sighs. "And *many* people worked on the same omnics and warbots that are now harming our world. Even Torbjörn Lindholm was at SST Laboratories once, before he started his crusade against AI. He was the visionary behind the very Bastions and Titans that you're fighting in the streets now.

"I know that people want me to apologize for what I did, but I can't."

The doors to the lab open, and they head inside. Chase thinks on Liao's words—she didn't know that Torbjörn was behind the Bastion and Titan units, but she's not surprised that he isn't publicizing it now. And Chase can't deny Liao's reasoning—but while she is grateful for some of Omnica's advances, what does it matter that they worked to improve the world if they also burned it to the ground?

As Liao finishes running diagnostics on Chase's new eyes, she shares what it was like growing up as a homeschooled prodigy in Singapore. Lonely years that Chase can relate to. Liao's father worked in the Chinese Academy of Sciences for a couple of years when she was younger. He was obsessed with alien life, talked for hours about what it would mean for humanity if they discovered another intelligence. But Mina Liao was interested in a different kind of intelligence.

"When I joined Omnica, I saw a chance to finally achieve my ambitions. I had grown up watching my father looking through the eyepiece of a telescope and asking, 'What would it mean if we weren't alone?' I had wondered too, longed to discover. That's what set me on my path," she says now. "Creating a sentient robot was like walking on the moon. I was part of it. Part of pushing mankind further."

Chase finds it hard to swallow her anger, though. "Is *this* further? We're standing on the brink of extinction—"

"I didn't expect it to end up this way either," Liao rushes in. "And no one takes this outcome harder than me. I wanted our discoveries to improve the world, not . . ." Liao's face is drawn, and she looks properly heartbroken when she asks, "But don't you have any regrets in your life, Vivian? Have you never hurt people you didn't mean to hurt? People you loved?"

Chase can't help but think about Bonnie in the thin light of the field hospital.

"Then you must understand too," Liao says, "what work it can take to try to forgive yourself."

3

OTTAWA

Even from the beginning, the location seems ambitious to Chase. Parliament Hill, the Crown lands on the south bank of the Ottawa River. The last time she was there, she was helping to evacuate the downtown area. Since then, she knows the omnics have rendered the place uninhabitable. A lot of the city now lies in ruin, and Chase is concerned that this central location will leave them exposed on all sides to attack.

"I know it's aggressive," Jack explains. "But in this war, we have to be. I'm sure you know these kinds of advances only buy us a few weeks of momentum before the omnics find a way to counter and we're back to the drawing board. But if Torbjörn and his team can set the Siege up here to begin with, it will give us a massive advantage in retaking the city fast. From there, we can expand the perimeter, reinforce it, hold it, move south."

"Sure," says Chase. "I understand that, but I'm concerned we don't have the resources to do this. We're already stretched thin, and if we lose here, we'll be stretched even thinner."

She suggested as much in the strategy meeting, but her warnings went unheeded against Jack's boundless optimism.

"We can't do it without a little risk, Chase," Jack says.

After they board the stratoscopter, Campbell briefs them on the campaign of air strikes that the RCAF are running ahead of them in order to clear the area. "Once you land," Campbell says over the comms, "your objective is to defend Torbjörn and his team for twenty minutes while they set up the Siege."

"Eighteen," Torbjörn corrects.

"And a half," Karlsson adds. "The turrets from the initial install can cover a few blocks, but we're going to need to install secondary bases in locations across the city."

Torbjörn nods. "We're hoping to use the ground gained, as well as the intelligence from the herons, to expand the perimeter from the center of the city and speed the removal of the omnics."

On the journey there, she's reviewing the moves in her head: where they'll disembark, where she'll direct her troops to maximize their chances. She's considering the strengths of each detachment and how best to utilize them. She's grown used to working with them over the past couple of months, but this is the first time that she'll be working with the thirty additional assaulters from the Overwatch team.

As soon as they land, she's on her feet, running, shouting directions over the comms. "Noah, you're defending our left flank. Zack, you and Mason on the right; use the high ground to your advantage. Snipers, into the center block, but be careful, the building's unstable. Get into formations," she shouts over the thunder of boots.

In less than a minute, all the troops are ready to deploy, flanking Torbjörn and the team of a dozen engineers who are working quick as they can to set up the Siege on the green in front of the Centennial Flame, the monument on Parliament Hill. Chase is close to the front line, at the crossing between Wellington Street and Metcalfe, scanning the area, ready to defend in the event of an attack.

Eighteen and a half minutes, Chase thinks. The air smells of sulfur and smoke. Despite the drizzle, fires are still burning from the bombing earlier. There are signs of the war all around, windows like full mouths of jagged teeth, fringed with shattered glass. The roofs of many of the buildings have caved in. There are cratered streets, overflowing gutters, and punctured manholes. But no omnics that Chase can see.

"The air strikes must have been more effective than we expected," Jack says over the comms.

"Robot barbecue." One of the Overwatch troops laughs.

Chase says nothing. She's not sure they'll be so lucky.

Another minute passes. Two.

Chase can see Parliament Hill in the reflection of her helmet's visor. It was always one of her favorite buildings, in one of her favorite styles—Gothic Revival. She has the Peace Tower, Canada's answer to London's Big Ben, in her sight. Last time she was here, she traveled with a school group up to the observation deck, where the sun-brightened prospect of Ottawa and Gatineau made her feel as if she could cover the world with her fist.

She never imagined she would one day return to evacuate the city. Or that she'd ever see the complex in this state of disrepair. The sight of it makes her think of London during the Blitz. The campanile is barely standing; the soot-blackened gargoyles and delicate friezes are half-crumbled or sunk in the mud.

"Sixteen minutes," an engineer's voice says over the comms. Then, "Fourteen."

The most subtle of movements catches Chase's attention. Some flicker on the other side of the Rideau Canal, among the half-felled hemlocks and beech trees. Chase wouldn't have seen it yesterday, with her old eyes.

"Get ready," she orders everyone.

"For what?" a couple of them whisper over the comms.

There is a feeling in the ground. Some subsonic rumble, the kind before an earthquake. Chase sees them first—from the hollow windows of the building, yellow lights like eyes appear. Then, sudden as grasshoppers, two OR14s lead a troop of ATW-Huntsman omnics—their spiderlike legs heavy enough to prick holes in the tarmac roads—lumbering down the street. There's only a moment before they open fire with their head-mounted cannons.

Her troops are ready and take aim at every omnic they can see. Chase lifts her rail gun and begins to shoot straight ahead at the next line of omnics: Bastions coming up Metcalfe Street, springing from the bombed-out rubble that was once a crêperie.

Chase manages to disable a few of the warbots with some

well-aimed rounds, but more crawl from the remains of buildings, or they plod heedlessly up the ruined streets. Others slide down dented trucks, easily taking fire hydrants, lampposts, and the alloy bodies of other robots in their gravity-defying stride.

"How much longer do we need to hold them off?" she shouts into her comm.

"Twelve minutes?" one of the engineers replies, but it sounds oddly like a question.

"Maybe if we're lucky," Chase mumbles as a hail of bullets fly at her troops. She can already see that they're outnumbered. Her soldiers have the positional advantage at the top of the hill, and it gives them a wide view of the army of warbots spilling from battered doorways, up O-Train passages, from under upturned cars. They are mainly Bastion E-54s and ATW-Huntsmen, but more OR14s are beginning to appear now in their ranks.

A rocket explodes, and she ducks for cover behind a bullet-pocked statue.

"I think we have five minutes," Chase shouts to Jack over the sound of gunfire. "Should we abort?"

On her right, Helena is coordinating on the comms while Noah is doing a great job of picking off the enemy from the second-floor window of the House of Commons. Firing and then ducking for cover, making himself a difficult target. Luca and Harper are on the front line, lobbing grenades to disrupt the omnics and hold them off for as long as they can. The Overwatch team is flanking them, covering as many angles as possible.

Jack is on the front line too, moving like Chase does in battle. He bobs and weaves past enemy fire, slaloming through obstacles. He'll find a good position to spray at the robots with his rifle, and when she blinks, he's vanished. His perfect aim and speed make Chase wonder, for the first time, if this is how he became a captain with Overwatch's strike team.

Jack launches a helix rocket at a group of oncoming Huntsmen and Bastions. It's only a second before they're torn to shreds by the explosion. Chase knows better than to celebrate the win, though; beyond the smoke, the lights of another fifty warbots wink at them from the dark crevices of the city.

"Chase," calls Avery from over the bridge, "you're not seeing what we're seeing."

Chase makes a motion with her eyes that overlays a map on her vision, and she can see her troops as stickmen icons, their positions highlighted even through buildings. Avery is on the other side of Parliament Hill, around the library. "On your six, there's a whole fleet of Bastions in tank configuration headed our way."

"Cover me," Chase shouts to Jack, slipping a little in the deep mud. Chase jumps from her hidden position and runs straight into the fray. An OR14 gets close enough to launch at a member of the Overwatch squadron with its superheated sword. The soldier can't dodge in time, and the sword lances right through his chest. With a wet cry, he falls heavily to the ground. The same OR14 turns then to swing for Chase, who is ready with her rail gun, firing enough rounds to completely disable it before it can hit her. When she looks up, there is another coming at her, but before she takes aim at it, it explodes into shards of scorched metal and polymers.

"Thanks," she says without turning to Jack. Ducking and weaving past fighters, Chase runs around to the other side of the

Parliament building, past the gorgeous library she used to love to look at, to a point where she can get a good vantage of the Alexandra Bridge.

Just as Sergeant Avery warned, there's a large squadron of Bastions rolling over the bridge, heading straight toward them. Maybe fifty warbots. Their armor makes them gleam like a school of fish. Chase shudders with contempt at the sight of them, but then eyes the bridge.

"Jack?"

"What is it, Chase?" A couple of feet behind her, he's unloading a storm of bullets at the OR14s climbing the hill.

"What's the range on your helix rockets?" She doesn't wait for his answer before asking, "Do you think you could hit that bridge?"

It takes another couple of rounds for Jack to dispatch with the omnic he's fighting. It's only then that he looks up, takes in the bridge in the few seconds he has before another energy sword careens his way.

"I've only got one left," Jack says, loading up his last rocket.

"Better make it count," Chase replies.

The bridge reflects off his blue visor. It's a tall structure, with five spans and steel trusses, almost six hundred meters long. On top, two lanes direct traffic either way; although, of course, the Bastion tanks are barreling up both lanes in one direction only.

A couple of the struts have already been damaged by previous air strikes. It's clear the structure is unsound. Chase's new acute vision is drawing her attention to the weakest areas; she picks one and asks him to aim for it.

"Worth a shot," he says, and launches his last helix rocket at the bridge. Chase bites her lip in anticipation. They know the plan has worked when a deep-throated growl echoes through the air and makes the river waters tremble. It's a sight to see, a real delight—the struts collapsing in on themselves, the concrete crumbling, whole chunks of it splashing into the dark waters, and then, wonderfully, the Bastions too, crashing like a tower of cards into the fast-moving river.

Both Jack and Chase let out a shout of triumph.

Jack smiles at her. "Good call, Chase."

Chase can't help but return the grin. "Nice shot, Jack."

It's enough to even the balance, to hold off the strongest robots at least long enough for Torbjörn and his team to set up the Siege.

"How long now?" Chase patches into them.

"We've run into a bit of trouble," one of the engineers says, his voice tremulous. "Two of our team have been injured."

Chase turns her cybernetic eyes on their position. While she was working to contain the situation on the bridge, two OR14s and a group of Bastions blew a hole in their flank. Sergeant Camille and her detachment are doing their best to hold them back, but they can't keep up the defense. Not when they're this out in the open.

"How long?" Chase repeats, dread twisting her stomach.

"I don't know," Torbjörn snaps.

"Your job was to keep them safe," Karlsson hisses over the comms.

"And their job was to set up this system fast. Do you know how many of my people I've lost out here?" Chase snaps back.

"It's okay," says Grayson. He and the CAF engineer sergeants are currently supporting the Overwatch team. "Give us maybe eight more minutes."

Chase unleashes a thunderstorm of bullets at the omnics in her path, leaping over trees and debris to draw their fire from her detachment.

But after a few moments of hope, the tide turns again. This was the problem she often ran into—a brilliant move that put a meaningful dent in the omnics' numbers inevitably led to a redistribution of enemy units. In a moment, the omnics would swarm her position as they're doing now, like bees to the hive, knowing one of their own is under attack. Her troops are overwhelmed, struggling to hold back the swelling tide of warbots. As soon as they destroy one set, a fresh troop comes pelting up the road or skittering like maggots from the empty eyes of buildings.

Hard to see, hard to focus, now, for the smoke and the sound of cannons. The smell of fire and blood.

Chase finds herself back where she started, on the now-muddied green in front of the Parliament building, when a Bastion in recon mode comes up to her with all the energy of a squall. It takes aim at her with a submachine gun. Chase dives just in time, out of the line of fire. Though the unit took her by surprise, she moves almost instinctively, firing her rail gun at the warbot's head enough times to watch it fall like Goliath into the mud.

Luca and Jensen lie prone in the mud. A projectile flies through the second-floor window of the House of Commons where Helena and Noah are working hard to keep the omnics back. It explodes with a sound that rattles Chase's bones. And for a breathless moment, she fears she's lost them too.

"Helena?" she calls over the comms.

"Here," her voice crackles.

Chase is trembling all over now, overwhelmed by the fight, by how many troops she's losing and how close she came to her own end. And then—her heart seizing in terror—she watches as a robot comes spiraling up the battlefield. She recognizes its motion from training videos and simulations, but she's never seen one in real life.

"Evacuate!" she orders her troops, Overwatch, and the engineers, signaling for the stratoscopter pilots to swing back around.

"What?" Jack is incredulous, furious. So is Torbjörn.

"We're almost finished!" Torbjörn shouts, his blond beard soaked in mud.

"That's a *Detonator*." Chase points in the distance, farther than normal eyes can see. It's an advanced combat unit that looks something like an old naval mine. It's coming at them with a swift, unswerving motion. Pre-Crisis, Detonators were utilized to demolish buildings in areas that weren't densely populated. Chase has watched one turn an entire factory into rubble.

"We only need four minutes," Grayson says, dismayed. Although Detonators are slow-moving, it's about three hundred meters away from where Chase is standing.

Judging by its speed, she says, "You've got two minutes to pack up."

At her order, her troops rush pell-mell toward the Library of

Parliament, where the stratoscopter's blades beat the air. Ninety seconds left. Chase stands behind them, keeping her heels planted firmly in the mud, making sure that as many of her soldiers as possible make it.

Some Bastion units rush after them. A soldier is hit, a line of bullets between his shoulder blades. Chase opens fire at the omnic's power core, and once it's destroyed, she runs over to help her fallen soldier. He is dead, though, lips black with blood.

"Sixty seconds," Chase shouts. The engineers are trying to figure out which components of their defense system they can take or leave behind. Overwatch doesn't want the omnics to recover any components of the new tech, but Chase reminds them everything in a three-mile radius will be ashes in thirty seconds.

If Chase doesn't run now, she won't make it. She does it under heavy omnic fire, ducking her head, vaulting the broken skeletons of gutted robots, shards of glass, and debris like hurdles. Her boots slide in the mud as she slows before the Library of Parliament. The stratoscopter is hovering near the cupola of its oxidized copper roof.

"Fifteen." Chase would give anything for a bit more time. For a chance to save everybody. Torbjörn and his team are heartbroken too: 120 more seconds was all they needed to finish setting up their defense system, to possibly turn the tide for Canada. But the robots were ready for them. A move ahead, every time.

Chase scrabbles quickly up a hanging cable as the stratoscopter is rising into the sky.

Five, four, three . . .

She won't make it inside in time, and so Chase braces herself, clutching the line tight.

Two, one . . .

An awful sound, a penetrating light. Chase feels her eardrums blow inward, and when she opens her eyes, she can hear almost nothing but ringing.

The stratoscopter raises them above the cloud of smoke, and she clings so tightly to the shuddering cable that it burns her palms. "Chase!" Helena leans over, squinting her eyes against the smoke as she helps to pull her captain up into the vehicle.

Chase is shivering and half-deaf inside stratoscopter. Medics are attending to the injured soldiers. Applying pressure to wounds or treating gunshots. Kai and Harper are both crying out in pain from their stretchers.

Chase gets unsteadily to her feet and rushes to the window.

"Don't do it." Helena puts her hand on Chase's shoulder. "It'll only upset you."

Chase goes anyway and regrets it. As the dust settles, she sees that the Parliament building has been almost completely destroyed, blown open, its roof vanished, exposing the structure inside: naked rooms, splinted struts, soot-stained carpets. Among the broken bodies of warbots are human soldiers, *her* soldiers. People she failed. People she's now left behind. She looks away to hide the tears in her eyes.

"How many?" she asks, but she's already looking at her troops and counting them: Helena, Noah, Mason, Avery . . .

"We don't know yet," Helena says. Her voice is shaking too. "It felt like an ambush."

"We could've seen it." Chase's despair curdles quickly into anger. "We *should* have expected it."

"You did, though," Jack says. "The attack and the Detonator. It was a good call, to evacuate."

"Yeah." Chase is grateful for her new eyes, how they aided her in battle, helped her to identify threats in the split second that can make all the difference on the battlefield.

"But still, not good enough." She glances over her shoulder at the smoke-darkened window.

They fly back, quiet with disappointment, and as the streets of Ottawa unspool below, Chase is thinking about the battle. And the next one, and the one after that. With the omnics guessing their moves, they can never afford to be so predictable again. They must attack where they are least expected, must surprise even themselves.

Chase is also thinking back to that morning. The way that Jack and her commanding officers dismissed her concerns. If it had been up to her, the mission would have turned out differently, might have been successful. Might have cost them less.

From her vantage, it looks as if the city belongs to the enemy. There is almost no sign of human activity—no cars moving, no lights on in any buildings, no children in the schoolyards or playgrounds, no people in the shops or restaurants. It grieves her heart to see it so transformed. Landmarks she once admired lie in ruins; museums, offices, and parking lots are bombed-out husks. She imagines alien archaeologists picking over the ruins of the city in another thousand years and concluding that their world always belonged to the robots. A chilling thought occurs to her; if they keep losing, it won't be long before the entire world looks like this.

"Brought you dinner." Jack's voice echoes. Chase looks up, still distracted. She's alone in the strategy room, her features lit by the projections from a dozen screens. She is so deep in thought, she doesn't hear him at first and has barely noticed that outside the sun has completely set.

"It's cold, but—"

"Thanks," she says without looking up. She hears the *shhh* of the tray sliding across the laminate surface of the table, and she can smell that it's chili . . . again. With the war affecting supply lines, their meals have become far more repetitive.

"Your troops say this is the place to find you, most nights."

"That's right," Chase says. Every night Chase watches simulated replays of the day's battle, imagining strategy, noting her troops' weaknesses and devising different formations to confound the omnics. The mistakes she's made—and the ones she still fears she'll make—haunt her sleep.

Jack leans against the opposite wall, keeping himself a little distant as he says, "Look, I should have spoken up more about this during the after-action report, but . . . we shouldn't have dismissed your concerns. You were right about the location. We were too exposed. That's why the mission failed."

Chase nods. She appreciates the acknowledgment.

"The strike team has never seen that many omnics," he admits. "And the way they fight—"

"It's because we're so close to the Detroit omnium," Chase says. He nods. "Right."

"It's different when you're this close to a strategic location for the omnics," she says. "They resupply their numbers faster, throw new variables at you faster."

"Well," he says as he steps closer and nods up at the monitor screens Chase has been examining: the layouts of the fights, her notes about omnic strategy. "I'd be grateful if you could fill me in a little more. Let me know what you've been up against here, what I should know about the fighting that maybe wasn't in any of the dossiers I received. Let me in on what you've been working on?"

With a wave of her hand, Chase conjures a couple of diagrams, visualizations of the omnic attack at the start of the Crisis. "It's strange," she says. "London, Lagos, Detroit, Toronto. The same strategy, at first. But now, each battle is different. They're learning the way we fight."

"But isn't that how they were built?" Jack asks.

"Of course," Chase says, frowning at the screen. "It's machine learning. They're designed to look for patterns in data and make better decisions depending on experience. But they discover our patterns pretty quickly, and then they're fast to adapt. I feel like I remember the week the war changed. The week they began to make a beeline for all our blind spots. Suddenly, wherever we were weakest, they were reinforced. And now . . ."

Now she's playing a game of Shah Matt against herself, trying to strategize at the same level of processing that created the problem. Only each piece is a real platoon, and the king is her country.

"The war reminds me of this game I used to play with my grandfather. It's a variation of chess." Heat flashes a little in her face; she feels embarrassed revealing this to him, as if the war were no more complex than a child's game.

"Chess," Jack muses. "You know, I used to play a lot myself."

"Oh yeah?"

"Yeah." He comes to sit on the edge of the table. "My uncle too, and his mother. Though he swore he'd never play again after '97. That was the year IBM invented a supercomputer called Deep Blue. You know, it beat Garry Kasparov—the world chess champion at the time—in a chess tournament."

Chase rolls her eyes. "Did you know that in 1969, three men landed on the moon?"

Jack laughs, a little embarrassed. "All right, sorry! Of course you know. My uncle always talked about it like the day some kind of innocence died."

"It was a milestone in the history of artificial intelligence." Chase's grandfather always said that.

"But what was it for *us*?" Jack asks.

"I don't know." Chase shrugs. "Humans invented Deep Blue. Mourning over it beating a human is like mourning over a race car beating a champion sprinter."

"I think it meant more than that," Jack argues. "Or, *he* did, anyway. Chess isn't like running—it's not a sport. It's an art. Deep

Blue won by brute force. It calculated millions of moves per second—the predictable, the terrible, and the absurd—every possibility to the problem until it alighted on the 'best,' most accurate solution."

"Accurate," Chase echoes. "Feels strange using that word in relation to chess."

"Exactly!" Jack says. "It's almost like asking, What's the most *accurate* brushstroke in a painting? What's the most *accurate* musical note?"

"True," Chase agreed. "Feels weirdly cynical. Or, I don't know, hollow."

"That's what my uncle worried. Still does. He complained for years that the game has become kind of cynical in the age of machines."

"Maybe he's right," Chase replies. "To win nowadays, you have to try to think like a machine. Choose the most logical moves, the most *accurate* moves over the beautiful ones."

"Beautiful?" Jack asks.

"Hmm." She leans forward and indicates her spreadsheets and diagrams. "Maybe, in trying to win this war, we've been trying too hard to think like a machine."

Chase looks back at the replaying footage before her. She is studying these moves to learn from the machines, but they are doing the same—studying her patterns to learn from her. An endless cycle of reaction. Maybe she needs to think more like her grandfather, to play the way he did.

"Not more logical," Chase says, a little smile curling the sides of her lips at the memory of his strategies. "More beautiful."

4

OLD TORONTO

The sunrise seems lovelier than usual. Chase isn't sure if the difference is her new eyes or the lasting effects of the prior night's insomnia. Perhaps it's simply relief at living to see another day. Chase is up before everyone else, on her own in the mess hall, watching as a band of garnet light billows over the snowcapped mountains. Crystalline spears of it are cast in all directions: salmon, sulfur, lemon.

The sound of footfalls on the linoleum makes her turn. It's Sergeant Noah, who looks as if he hasn't slept much either, holding something tight in a fist.

"Bad night?" she asks.

"They're all bad at the moment."

Chase nods grimly as he comes to sit opposite her, and her

eyes pick out the red capillaries against the whites of his eyes, the sallow purple shadows under them.

"What have you got?" Chase nods at his balled fist, and Noah smiles a little. Places it on the table between them. She thought it was an apple for a moment, but now she sees it's a pomegranate. It might as well be a rock plucked from a crater on the moon.

With supply lines totally disrupted by the war, and the harsh Canadian winter, it's been weeks since she's seen fresh fruit, let alone eaten any. She wants to say, "Wow." She wants to peel it open and pluck its tiny seeds.

"Where did you get it from?" she asks. Noah taps the side of his nose.

"A man's gotta keep his sources secret." Then he leans forward. "It's a gift."

"For Helena?" Chase teases.

Noah blushes a little, lowers his gaze. "I guess I'm not so good at keeping secrets after all."

"No," she says. "Not much in this detachment gets by me." Noah is still looking away, and she can see from the shadows flitting across his face that he's steeling himself to say something.

"I'm going to ask her to marry me."

"That's wonderful, Noah." Chase leans over to give him a quick hug. "The best news I've heard all day."

"It's still morning." He laughs, then says, "Yeah," as if psyching himself up for the task.

She asks, "Is a pomegranate the right . . . ?"

"Well, I could hardly buy a ring," he says.

Chase thinks of her sister's opal ring she never had the chance to give back. It's among her belongings still. She used to imagine giving it back to her when the war is over.

"But I keep thinking," Noah continues, "is now the time? Should I wait for all this to pass? We were on and off before the Crisis, and now—"

"*Now*"—Chase puts her hand on his shoulder—"is as good a time as any. A better time."

Then the breakfast bell rings, and they are startled to attention. Hoisted into the hurly-burly of the day.

After breakfast, Chase's detachments gather in the strategy room with the Overwatch troops. Chase is excited to explain the concept of operations that she's devised and her commanding officers have signed off on. This time, Chase collaborated with Jack and the engineering team to choose a less exposed location in Toronto to set up the Siege, but one that is central enough to give them good coverage. Together, they chose Spadina Road: the section that runs like a bridge over a downtown park. It's in an area of Toronto where relatively little omnic activity has been detected recently. If the engineers set the Siege up in the middle of the bridge, it will form a natural choke point that her soldiers can defend on either side. The location and position will decrease the chances of them being overwhelmed.

She believes they will have better luck in Toronto, as it's somewhere the omnics won't expect, but after their failed mission in Ottawa, she has labored for a long while on different contingency plans in case they need to evacuate the area.

Chase presents it to the group now, standing before the large projector screen, enlarging the map of the city and various escape routes. There is a tension among her detachment members she can still sense. A certain wariness.

"What if we see another Detonator unit?" one of them asks.

"Air support will be poised for a quick evacuation," Chase explains, "but I've considered both air and ground evacuations, since this mission is much farther behind enemy lines."

She's gone through the plan with her own brute-force calculations. "The ground evacuations." The projection flips to an animation of the formation and troop movement—with her forces dispersing in a sort of star shape to scatter any omnics pursuing them, then reconvening in Davenport House, which is in one of the least-hit areas of the city. If everyone manages to disable or outrun the omnics on their tail, it should give them some time to evacuate into the suburbs, where air support will be waiting for them.

"It's funny," Helena says, the light of the projection flashing across her retinas, "the way your formations look. The timing of the troop movement compared to the projected omnic response is a little like a dance, here. Kind of symmetrical—"

"Logical," Grayson says.

"No," Jack says. "Beautiful."

Chase smiles. She's pleased when Commanding Officer Fournier congratulates her on the plan. She's also satisfied seeing the tension among the troops turn to tentative confidence.

Before they leave, Chase heads down to the armory with Noah, Grayson, and the engineers. Overseeing them loading the stratoscopter. The room is almost empty when her attention is caught by two voices in one of the neighboring rooms, the door ajar.

"Doesn't it make sense for me to be there? In case anything goes wrong?" Chase recognizes Liao's voice, lowered but tense.

Torbjörn huffs. "Nothing will go wrong that we can't handle."

"*We?*"

"The team cleared for combat missions. Which doesn't include you."

"I just—" she begins.

"No need to be so pessimistic," Torbjörn continues, snapping together one of his holsters. "We have a great team. And a good plan. Isn't that right, Chase?"

Chase starts, embarrassed to be caught eavesdropping. "Right," she says with a cough.

It's been a couple of months since she left her city. Toronto looks different already, covered in heavy drifts of snow. No snowplows or winter service vehicles means that the roads and avenues are like frozen rivers. One advantage of the snow is that it's easy to see where the omnics have passed through recently. Chase is reassured that there are no signs of movement on the segment of Spadina Road elevated above Winston Churchill Park. But it's also strange not to see it full of dog walkers or commuters, children all bundled up throwing snowballs.

Chase is sure that once they land, any omnics nearby will be alerted to their presence. They always seem to know when her forces are approaching.

The blades of the stratoscopter spin the snow in wild vortices below. Chase is one of the first off the ramp and into the snow, which is nearly half a meter deep and will be exhausting for her detachments to wade through. As she cuts a path, she's grateful for the extra strength her cybernetics provide.

Chase has heard that Torbjörn practiced drills with the engineers overnight, trying to maximize their efficiency and shorten the Siege setup time.

"Fifteen minutes," Grayson says. When she looks back at him, he's already started typing furiously into his data pad.

"Move out," Jack commands. Chase gestures for her detachments to set up in their positions.

It takes less than three minutes for the omnics to find them and attack their location. But Chase's plan seems to have caught them off guard. They're far fewer in number than what they encountered in Ottawa, and it's easy to hold them off from the bridge, where each detachment only needs to be wary of attack from one direction.

As Torbjörn's team counts down five minutes, then four, Jack's and Chase's teams make easy work of the oncoming Bastions, Huntsmen, and smattering of OR14s. Chase allows herself a brief moment to hope that they might make it this time.

"Okay," Torbjörn says over the comms, "looking good."

"One minute," Grayson says, his jaw trembling a little in the cold.

Chase can feel something shift under her boots.

"Torbjörn, is that you?" she asks him.

"Is what me?"

But in the next moment everyone is looking around in terror as a loud crash of trees falling tears the air.

A thought flashes through Chase's mind, a terrified suspicion, a worst-case scenario, but she tries to squash it.

"Almost there," Torbjörn says.

"Fifteen seconds," Grayson counts down.

"Air support," Chase whispers into her comm.

"Yes, Captain?"

"Be ready for a quick evacuation." Their stratoscopter is hovering low over Winston Churchill Park.

"Nine," Grayson counts.

But they all see it, in the same awful moment. Rising from the trees like those old videos Chase used to watch of *kaiju* rending the Tokyo skyline.

"A Titan," she says, then curses under her breath. "It's always something."

"Seven."

Chase has nightmares of these machines. A bipedal omnic twenty stories high, originally designed to help in the construction of high-rises, dams—massive construction projects that require inhuman strength.

But the omnics have turned it into a giant, magnificent weapon, fortified with enormous firepower, triple-barreled grenade launchers, arm-mounted energy cannons . . . She watched a video of Australia's armed forces trying to take one down in Sydney as the monster crashed into three skyscrapers, leveled buildings, and flattened cars, all while repelling anything the military threw at it.

"We need to evacuate," she says, but she's having trouble standing, the ground is shaking so violently now.

"The Siege will increase our firepower," Torbjörn insists stubbornly.

Chase can't imagine a few drones and turrets will do much against this behemoth. Even ones created by the greatest scientific minds humanity can muster.

"Two."

Chase is holding her breath. She knows how it's supposed to look when the Siege initiates, so she braces for the moment that the herons take to the sky and the turrets begin firing.

"One."

Nothing happens. Everyone is still, waiting for it. Torbjörn's voice comes over the comms, "Was the initiation sequence off count?"

Chase is counting upward in her head at that moment when the Titan storms them and launches a missile into the road. It smashes through cement and snow; the troops nearby scatter.

Then it launches another missile at the stratoscopter, now approaching at her command. Chase watches in terror as their only means of escape spirals out of the sky and explodes into gouts of flame.

Chase's heart plunges in her chest. "Torbjörn, pack up what you can and get ready to move, now."

Time to go. In only a few seconds, they could all be dead. But she's imagined almost everything and has a contingency plan.

"Ground evacuation," she shouts over the comms, and her soldiers erupt into action.

Everyone close to the engineers helps to lift or wheel the Siege components.

The Titan aims a missile that makes another cavity in the road. Chase ducks for cover as the ground rumbles, snow and debris bursting around her. She rolls out of the way of a flying shard of steel. As black smoke rises, Chase sees that half the bridge has been destroyed. Noise, furious chaos, the sound of her soldiers as they flee in all directions, hoping to confuse the omnics and diffuse their fire.

But there is a body on the other side of the bridge, helmet knocked off. At the sight of her copper curls, Chase's heart lurches.

"Helena!" Noah shouts, but there is a scorched chasm between them, and the Titan is launching another missile. No way to get to her without certain death.

On an impulse, Chase grabs Noah. Just in time, as another strike lands. The ground behind them crumbles, and more of the bridge falls into the park below. She saved his life, but Chase knows that he won't see it that way.

"*That's Helena!*" he shrieks into the black smoke rising around them.

"She's gone, Noah," Chase says. "We need to keep moving."

But Noah is on his knees, jaw clenched in pain.

"Noah!"

Another missile explodes near them, snow, dust, and shrapnel flying at their faces. He's half-buried now in the ground. "I'm not going without you," she says, taking him by the shoulders and pulling him to his feet.

The ground rumbles under them, and the voices of the detachment commanders shouting over her comms is barely audible under the ringing in her ears.

"You will evacuate to Davenport House, and that's a direct order, Sergeant!" she shouts at him.

They run together, then. Taking the route that Chase plotted, in a roundabout way that skirts Spadina Road, the snow making their strides ungainly.

By the time they're on the edge of Castle View Avenue, Chase and Noah run headlong into two OR14s, which she dispatches easily with her rifle.

Chase can see the directions her soldiers have run from the footsteps on the pavement, but the snowstorm and ash will soon cover them. They seem to be following her plan, rushing helter-skelter in all directions. Anyone following the trail might not decipher that the prints all convene on Davenport House, the historic mansion museum in downtown Toronto.

Chase promised Bonnie for years she would take her on a day trip here, but she never managed to—a thought that stings with regret now.

Her breath catches at the sight of the place: a Gothic Revival–style mansion, former home of a financier. From the bottom of Davenport Hill, it rises like a fantasy castle above the snow, all frosted turrets and battlements. Although she's never visited herself, when Chase devised this plan, she considered how its position and architecture might make it easy to defend. It's in an area of low omnic activity, and she'd imagined its hidden underground tunnels could make for good places to wait out an air strike or escape a siege.

"Noah." She turns to him before they get inside. But the look on his face, the pain in his eyes when he turns to her, stops her short. He simply shakes his head and storms off in a different direction. She stands for a moment, wondering if she should follow after him, but then she turns and sees that most of her detachments have gathered inside the house and are waiting for her direction.

It's a relief to see her troops in the great hall of the museum, catching their breath on the velvet chairs or sprawled on the lacquered floor. Some tussle must've taken place out on the terrace a while ago, because most of the glass in the forty-foot bay window is shattered. The evacuation went exactly as she'd planned. They were able to get out on time, with far fewer casualties than last time and no Titan crashing after them. In spite of everything, Chase is proud of her team right now.

The ground is littered with sparkling shards that crunch underfoot, while icy wind blasts snow into the room, tossing ghostly cyclones across the floor. It looks like an ice palace, with crystal stalactites hanging from broken chandeliers.

The engineers have managed to wheel most of their equipment inside and stand, now, in a huddle, their voices raised, arguing about what to do next.

Jack is doing a roll call of the Overwatch troops, who are pink-cheeked and breathless, bright plumes of condensation blowing from their nostrils. A couple cry out in pain as others tend to their wounds.

Chase doesn't need to call names to know who she's lost.

"Helena?" Avery asks. "Anyone seen her?"

Chase shakes her head, dreading to think of the way Noah looked on the bridge, his face an all-too-familiar mask of grief. Compared to how he had looked that morning, brimming with love and pride at the thought of marrying Helena.

"We're missing three more. Where's Jake?"

"I saw him in the library," one detachment member says.

"The others . . . ?" someone else ventures.

"The others might turn up yet," Jack says, ever the optimist.

But the mood in the room is grim. *Another failed mission,* Chase thinks, a bitter taste in her mouth. All in spite of her meticulous planning, her change in approach.

"What happened?" She turns now to Torbjörn, who stands on the threshold, his jaw tight with a frustration and rage they all share.

"The initiation sequence . . . the turrets failed to engage."

"I thought you practiced this," Chase says through gritted teeth, trying and failing to hide her own frustration.

"At the moment," says Sergeant Grayson, his clothes blackened with smoke, "we're thinking that some of the components were damaged in transit."

"*Thinking?*" Jack says.

Torbjörn swears under his breath. "We'll need to do an inventory to confirm. Then we can assess whether or not we can fix it here."

"The mission isn't over, though," says Grayson. "Once we fix it, we could set it up on this end of Spadina Road. It's not that far from our original target."

"Even if we do fix it," Chase says, "we need something that gives us enough firepower to destroy a *Titan*."

"Well, you're looking at it," Torbjörn says. Although Chase finds this hard to believe, as she's never seen any of the components of the system in action before, she is willing to defer to Torbjörn's assessment. Especially considering, it occurs to her now, that he designed the Titans himself and understands intimately how they operate.

"How long will it take to find and fix the bug in the Siege?" Jack asks.

"A couple of hours."

An audible sigh erupts from the gathered soldiers.

"We've also lost our way home," Chase says. "I'll need to radio back to the base for them to send another stratoscopter. And even then, they likely won't confirm it until that Titan is out of the picture."

"We'll probably need to last the night, then," Jack says, like a doctor delivering a miserable prognosis. "Like you said, this place is easy to defend. Gives time for the engineers to sort out their issue."

"Makes sense, since we don't have many hours of daylight, at the moment," Chase says. None of them like the idea of setting up the Siege at night. Especially since a confrontation in the dark gives the omnics an advantage over her soldiers; IR vision can only do so much to level the playing field.

Chase grits her teeth. "First things first: secure the area." She splits them up and tells them which floors and directions to cover—stables, secret passages, the tunnels. They need to root out and disable any omnics that might be hiding in the grand location.

"On the bright side," Jack says dryly, "can't beat these accommodations."

There are a couple of chuckles of agreement before everyone disbands.

Like Jour de Chance, the historic houses did not employ much omnic assistance, so the place looks frozen in time . . . except for the cold air flurrying in through the broken windows.

As Chase strides through the oak-paneled halls, her soldiers patch in. "All clear in the servants' quarters."

"Conservatory clear."

"The study."

"The smoking room."

"I'm in the tower, and I can't see anything."

Chase kicks open the door to a room. A little display tells her it's the lady of the house's quarters. She proceeds through a suite of rooms with her rifle upright, finally arriving at the bedroom. It has Wedgewood-blue walls and a four-poster bed, though the floorboards are splattered with mold and algae clings to a stream of water pouring from a cracked pipe. Chase's boots make wet prints on the thick rugs.

Chase regards her reflection, split seven ways in the golden overmantel. Evidence of her sleepless night is visible in the lines under her eyes. She sits on the golden comforter and radios back to the base, explaining what happened. It causes her almost physical pain to relive the details. She wants to say, *I did everything right.*

"Another failed mission," Campbell says over the comms. Maybe it's her current low mood, but Chase finds it easy to imagine some ledger in his mind, a detailed log of her mistakes.

"It's not over yet," she tells them. "Grayson says the Overwatch engineers need two hours to fix the bug. Requesting permission to set up the defense system in a new location, near our current position."

"That's bound to draw the attention of the Titan. And maybe more omnic fire."

"I understand that, sir," Chase says, "but we think we can hold it off long enough to install the system. If it works—"

"That's the crux, though, isn't it? *If it works.*"

Chase grits her teeth. She has no control over whether or not the defense system comes back online. But she can choose to trust the people she works with and believe that they will do everything they can.

"If it works," she continues, "we'll need a swift evacuation."

"This is Warrant Officer Duvall with Special Operations Aviation Squadron," a new voice cuts in. "We can dispatch evac tomorrow morning at oh-six-hundred hours to retrieve you, but the area is crawling with omnics armed with antiaircraft weaponry. We can't enter until a perimeter is secured by the Siege, or you can rendezvous at a new, secure location. Understood?"

"Copy that. Thank you," Chase says. She knows it's all she can hope for after what happened to their pilot earlier that day. CSOR have limited resources, and they can't afford to risk the safety of another crew by flying into an area with Titan activity.

Her nerves feel frayed at the end of the call, and she lies for a while on the bed. As she does, the voices of the engineers float up through the open window, although a lot of the technical language goes over her head. She can hear Torbjörn's low rumble, Grayson's reply. Jack shouting from the balcony. She takes her helmet off and rubs her eyes.

Jack was right: this might be the nicest place that Chase has ever spent the night, and as the hours pass, morale increases. At first it looks as if they're in for a dinner of nuts, energy bars, and dehydrated glucose drinks. But then some of the detachment members raid the kitchen and find tinned fruit marzipan and chocolate.

They spread out through the grand house, raiding the library or sleeping on the four-poster beds. A couple set up a ball game in the smoking room.

"According to the brochure," Avery says, "the carved molding in the Oak Room took three artisans three years to carve."

Chase lets out a low whistle.

She sets up a rotation for watch and takes the first shift, doing a tour of all the rooms and halls and then around the grounds, glad that her infrared vision can help her to easily detect activity in the trees or out on the road.

But in the quiet hours she can't help but wonder, *Where is the Titan?* Imagining the amber glow of its visual sensors looming over some bridge uptown. Waiting for any sense of their location to begin its destruction.

At the end of her watch, Jack finds her in the conservatory, doing what she always does: considering the next day's fight.

Although it's harder to do without the consoles and displays. The thought of the battle to come disturbs her peace.

The room is like a church hall, with gorgeous tall windows and a colorful stained-glass ceiling that is mostly intact. A rainbow cascade of lights scatter all around. She is staring at the checkered pattern on the Italian marble floor. It looks like a Shah Matt board.

"Hey," Jack says, his breath like smoke in the subzero temperatures. Down the hall, she can hear some of the Overwatch troops talking low.

"This was a good choice." He nods, looking around. "And your evac plan worked perfectly."

"Yeah," Chase says, "though, obviously, I was hoping we wouldn't have to rely on it."

Jack looks out at the cloud-shrouded moon and says, "Do you ever sleep?"

"Not lately," Chase admits, rubbing her eyes. She's always wondered if her cybernetic body handles sleep deprivation better than her old one did. "And not tonight."

It's freezing, and the troops they lost are all on her mind. How Helena looked on the bridge. The despair in Noah's voice as he shouted for her. Perhaps Jack can tell from the shadows in Chase's expression what is bothering her.

"I haven't been able to get them off my mind either," he admits, coming to sit beside her and stare out the tall window.

"It's always like this for me," Chase says without looking at him. "I always wish . . ." She shakes the thought away.

"They knew the risks when they joined this fight. Just as you did."

Chase hates this line, always has. Could she give those words to Helena's family? To Noah? Can she carve them into any tombstone?

"As captain, my job is to bring my people home," she says. "I want to trust Torbjörn, but what if this Siege system never works? What do I say to their parents, their *kids*? What do I say to—"

"It's hard, isn't it?" Jack cuts in. "Being in this position when you're augmented. It's like you have this superpower—you can see the danger coming, but you don't have the power to protect them from it. I know, Chase." He puts a hand on her shoulder. "And I also know this wasn't your fault."

"Are you—" Chase looks up at him, recalling the sight of him in Ottawa, the way he fought, how fast he could run, the lightning-flash of his reflexes. "Augmented?"

Jack smiles. "Sort of. I was part of the US military's Soldier Enhancement Program."

She was somewhat disappointed to hear it. She hoped he was cybernetic—had some of the same experiences as her—but his words are still surprising. Before the Crisis, she believed that the program was an urban legend. It sounded ridiculous: an American governmental agency, conducting controversial experiments on top soldiers in the military. The scientists used genetic engineering to increase the speed, strength, and endurance of their human volunteers. But after the Crisis broke out, they expanded the recruitment pool and the program was confirmed to be more than myth.

"Yeah." He smiles a little at her surprise. "If you had told young me, Jack at eighteen, simple farm kid I was, that I'd be chosen to become an 'enhanced soldier,' I would have laughed, probably. My childhood was so different from all this." He gestures around. "Rural Indiana. Up at the crack of dawn to help my father muck stalls." He talks about it with nostalgia, a wistful glitter in his eye.

"It sounds nice," Chase says.

"It was. I couldn't wait, though, to turn eighteen and enlist."

"Me neither," Chase says. "It's in my blood."

"I hear that. I was first sergeant when the Crisis broke out. It changed everything. That's when I was recruited into the Soldier Enhancement Program."

"What was . . . that like?" Chase asks tentatively. "I heard that hundreds of soldiers volunteered."

"Most of them died," Jack says, staring ruefully into the distance, his brow furrowed. "I made it. But it wasn't a pleasant journey. Injections, unbelievable pain. I think I had a surgery at one point, when some of my organs were rejecting the changes . . . I was in and out of a coma for a few weeks. I'm not sure I'll ever know the full extent of what was done, or what it might do to me over time."

Chase knows well what it's like to wake up in a different body. To learn to walk again. To trust it. Jack tells her how his new body is faster and stronger. His wounds heal quickly, and he needs less sleep. They still don't know what other changes might be in store for him—how his body will react to illness and age.

Chase stares at him now with a new kind of recognition. Not quite fellowship, but something akin to it. Jack's biological enhancements came at a cost, as her cybernetic augmentations had. They set him apart, even as they lent him some physical advantages over his comrades.

"I'd do it again," he says. "All of it. Even knowing what I know . . ." He trails off for a little bit. "And Overwatch too. I was—am—happy to don that blue uniform."

"Really?" she asks. Would Chase do it all again? Knowing what she does? Volunteer to stand in the thinning phalanx that separates the human race from total destruction? The war with no end in sight?

"I know that volunteering for the program, the abilities they gave me, make a difference, not just for me but for the people I fight with."

Chase nods. "In Ottawa, my enhanced eyes noticed the Detonator before anyone. I know I saved lives back there, but that doesn't make it easier when I lose them."

"That's because you're a good leader, and you're going to get through this. We all will. Torbjörn and Liao are the best technological minds humanity has. There aren't many problems they can't solve—"

He stops talking when Chase leaps to her feet with a gasp.

"Liao!" she says to his quizzical look.

Chase races out to the engineering team, where the energy seems to be at a low ebb. She can tell already that they haven't had the success they expected, fixing the Siege. They're surrounded by machinery, tools, wires, and data pads. Torbjörn is talking gravely to a group of them, huddled around a turret.

"Torbjörn?" Chase asks, drawing him aside. He looks like a snowman in his winter whites. "Have you discussed these issues yet with Dr. Liao? That day, before Ottawa—we came by the armory, and you discussed the initiation sequence with her . . . She might have a solution you haven't thought of yet."

He huffs, and his breath comes like a gout of smoke from his nostrils. "We had an agreement: turrets, my team; herons, her. She doesn't know anything about my work—"

"I think she knows more about your work than most people in this room," Chase says with a discerning look.

She can tell that the thought of letting Dr. Liao in makes him uneasy, and she understands. She's had her own misgivings about the doctor and her history, but if Chase hadn't relied on her to help fix the injury to her lens, who knows what condition her eyes would be in.

"We trust you, Torbjörn. That's why we're willing to put our lives on the line for your defense system. We have to trust one another, because none of us can win this war alone."

Crouching for warmth near the entryway, Sergeant Grayson looks up at Overwatch's chief engineer, almost bracing for a reprimand as he forms the words. "At this point, anything is worth a try, right?"

"All right, all right," he says with another heavy breath. "Get a comms sergeant over here and we can see what she has to say."

Chase watches nervously as Torbjörn and the engineers make contact with Liao. She notes the polite tension between the two of them as the doctor lists the components she thinks may have failed and how they can reroute the electronics to allow the system to work without them.

A lot of the conversation isn't easy to follow. Chase can pick up a few bits—some terms she understands because of her own cybernetics—but the exchange moves too quickly. A couple of hours before sunrise, Chase finds herself falling asleep by the fireplace in the great hall, their voices floating around her.

But at five a.m., Chase is woken by shouts from the team of engineers gathered on the terrace.

"Genius," Grayson is saying as Chase approaches.

The sun is only just beginning to rise, so everyone is bathed in deep-blue light.

"What is it?" Chase asks. The team points out the machine at the end of the lawn, riding through the snow like a tank.

"A thing of beauty," Torbjörn says, squinting as he stares out at the turret.

"She did it," one of the engineer sergeants says.

"*We* did," says another, rubbing his eyes in a way that betrays his sleepless night.

"It works?" Jack asks, hanging back in the doorway with a yawn. Chase can tell that Jack too is hopeful.

"Looks like!"

"Though, it's one thing here," Torbjörn says. "It's another thing out *there*."

It almost feels as if they're all holding their breath when her troops set up in a new formation in Spadina Park, poised to defend the engineers from attack. Chase finds herself near the Baldwin Steps, everything in her still, listening out for the sound of the Titan.

Torbjörn and the engineers work quickly, setting up the Siege in the middle of the park. Their activity will have caught the attention of any warbots nearby.

Chase is hoping that they'll have enough time before the Titan approaches to initiate the Siege, which—according to Torbjörn—will provide enough firepower to defeat it, allowing them to make a quick escape before they are surrounded.

"We're close," Grayson says over the comms. "Two minutes."

Better be two minutes, Chase thinks grimly, because she can feel the ground beginning to shake under her boots. The sound of the Titan marching toward them makes her bones rattle and her jaw clench. Her soldiers point their weapons in the direction of the rumbling.

"One minute."

Snow shakes loose from the trees and birds scatter away. In Greek mythology, Titans were the first race of gods. *An apt name,* Chase thinks, *for what a giant it is.* It levels buildings as it passes, flattens trees, leaves craters in the ground where it steps.

Then the Titan is on them, rising like a space shuttle into view, and they all begin firing. Jack is the first to try to disable it, hurling helix rockets at its head, but that only seems to enrage it, not slow it down. All the soldiers take aim, though most bullets bounce off its armor like peanuts against a chalkboard.

"Thirty seconds."

Can they hold off this colossus for even that long? Their combined fire seems to be slowing it down only a little. It launches a missile in Chase's direction, and she dodges, watching it explode in the snow, flinging debris and wooden splinters from the trees everywhere. Chase must squint her eyes to avoid being blinded. Sergeant Mason cries out in pain, and she can see him, limp on the snow.

"Twenty."

Another explosion, and then another.

Chase gives a command to one of the assaulters and orders them to fire off grenades. Chase watches as the weapons burn a hole in the Titan's armor. They don't look as if they deal quite as much damage in this weather, but they're enough to hold the Titan back for a couple more seconds. All the seconds they need.

"Ten," shouts Grayson. "Nine!"

Chase's heart is in her throat. She can see from the plumes of condensation in the cold air that no one is taking a breath. A repeat of yesterday's failure to initiate will give the Titan enough time to kill them all.

"Four."

Chase has to fight every urge in her body not to run from the path of the oncoming warbot.

"Three."

She plants her feet on the ground and hopes.

"Two."

If it works, the combined firepower of Torbjörn's turrets and the herons' intelligence should turn the tide of their battle, but it could also give them a chance in the entire war.

"One."

With a sound like a rocket launching, the herons leap into the gray dawn. There is a collective cry of exhalation over the comms as, with simultaneous jolts and clunks of metal, the turrets engage, light up, and begin to fire.

It's magnificent to watch. The mechanical ballet of the herons ducking and weaving below the clouds, their sensors drawing a picture of omnic activity and relaying the 3D image immediately back to the turrets, which roar to life with a sound like thunder. All the troops duck out of the way as the long range turrets barrel ahead on all terrain treads and begin to unleash an astonishing amount of damage into the Titan.

At first, Chase feels a flush of satisfaction at the sight of the thing meeting its match. With each well-aimed shot from the turrets, the giant sheds scraps of machinery, metal, and armor, which crash to the ground. She's so busy staring it takes a second for Chase to realize that she's in danger of being hit. When she looks around, all her soldiers are diving for cover under the trees or a good distance away, near the museum.

The Titan shudders and stumbles. Sparks fly from its chest, erupt inside its head. It feels like watching a piñata smashed to bits by gleeful partygoers. Almost too much, Chase thinks at the smoke and destruction. From the way Torbjörn is smiling, she can tell he thinks it's just enough.

Then, the heels of the great machine begin to sway. *It's going to fall,* Chase thinks with a flash of panic, *and when it does, it will crush everyone under it.*

"Run!" she shouts. Everyone flies away from the park as fast as they can. In the distance, Chase can hear the beating of stratoscopter blades—their ride home.

Chase rushes to Sergeant Mason, who is clutching his side

where a shard of shrapnel has pierced him. "You'll be okay," she says, lifting him into her arms and running.

Her troops and Overwatch pelt ahead of them, their feet smashing through the snow. At the foot of the ramp, two other detachment members haul Mason up. Chase stays by the entrance to help everyone in—Avery, Grayson, Camille, Noah, Jake—to make sure they've all made it, as the turrets continue their assault and the air fills with the smell of ozone and smoke.

They're flying when they see it. With an enormous whine of machinery, the Titan falls to its knees and then crashes like a cannonball into a lake, the snow flying up in huge drifts around it.

Victory.

Chase can hardly believe it. She's dizzy with disbelief. Victory, on the heels of so much defeat. Everyone is cheering, shouting, singing the national anthem or the theme song to the movie that's been playing on repeat in the base's common room.

Jack says, "We'll need to send in more detachments to expand the perimeter. If we can cover all of Toronto with a couple of installations around the city, it will be like having our own satellite army down there now. Able to fight twenty-four seven. We'll need to keep the momentum going before they can find a way around the Siege. But if we do, we can take back Toronto and the other cities."

"Yeah." It's been a long time since she's smiled so much. Chase is heady with delight at their success, and grateful for Overwatch's help. For their firepower and resources, for Torbjörn and Liao. She feels something else too, something unfamiliar. A glimmer of it at the realization that if they keep going this way, they might actually be able to turn the war around.

Hope.

5

LAURENTIDES

"Looks great to me," Liao's voice chimes brightly from outside the scanner.

Chase steps out, rubbing the scratches and tears in the silicone gloves that cover her prostheses.

When Chase had first been fitted for her prosthetic arm, she expected the silicone skin to be cold. She'd been surprised to feel that the motors and mechanics made it warm—one of the many marvels of her cybernetic body she so seldom thought twice about over the years.

"They're only cosmetic," Liao says of the cuts. On one of the monitor screens is a 3D reconstruction of Chase's body—turning slowly like DaVinci's *Vitruvian Man*. She is surprised to discover that something has shifted in her. She used to wince at the sight of those images, but today . . . today she is unapologetically *proud*. Her body is a marvel. A noble tool, the thing that saved her.

"There are Prosthetics artists who can fix the skin for you, but I'm no artist," Liao says. She stares down at Chase's arm. Something has nicked the silicone, revealing the metal underneath, a sliver of silver, like the edge of a dime. Chase isn't sure how it happened. Maybe flying shrapnel during their frantic escape from the falling Titan. "It's not so bad," she says. A month ago, staring at the dings would have bothered her, would have made her feel other. Today she sees them as well-earned scars from yesterday's battle, and the one she's been fighting all her life.

"It's lucky," Chase says, pulling the sleeve down. "I mean, I was." She's thinking of Helena, in the path of an oncoming missile. And Noah, how he looked, then and now, haunted by grief. She hasn't been able to bring herself to talk to him yet. Sergeant Mason too was in bad shape when the medic reached him. Chase was relieved to hear that he's stable now, though.

"I've been thinking, actually," Chase muses, sitting on one of the melamine chairs on this side of the room. "About how to make more luck."

"Oh?" the doctor says, her eyes flashing with intrigue.

"Yeah," Chase continues. "I've been reflecting on the people we lost and what could have been done to save them. What I'm capable of doing . . . In battle, sometimes the difference between life or death comes down to a fraction of a second, or the moment on a weapon, the trajectory of a bullet. If there's something I can do to improve my chances even a little, shouldn't I do it?"

"Right," Liao says with a knowing smile.

She hadn't been sure before. Hadn't trusted Liao enough or been ready to fully embrace her cybernetics as more than the everyday tools that helped her even the playing field. But now. "The other enhancements you were talking about. The upgrades to make me faster and stronger," she says. "I think I'm ready to hear more about them."

Before Liao can reply, though, there's a pounding on the door that makes her start, almost dropping her data pad.

"Torbjörn!" she exclaims as she opens it. "Have you ever done anything quietly?"

"Once," he says, and strides in, looking about the room. The three of them are alone. He acknowledges Chase with a nod, and then, as if he's been holding his breath, he turns to Liao.

"I just came back from speaking to Campbell," Torbjörn says.

"Oh." Liao's expression hardens.

The energy between Chase's team, Overwatch, and all the engineer sergeants was high that afternoon, during the after-action report. Everyone who had been on the mission was excited about the win, about watching the Titan destroyed and the successful installation of the Siege. Chase noticed a chill amongst the commanding officers, though. It seemed as if they were still disconcerted by the defense system's initial failure. None more so than Major Campbell. Although he didn't overtly voice his concerns, Chase heard as much from her sergeants. Avery even said Campbell had been discussing his misgivings about the herons for more than a week with Fournier. He believed that they were inherently flawed and dangerous. Chase couldn't help but take his words a step further, though, and wondered if he was actually sowing doubt about Liao.

"I made it clear to him," Torbjörn says now, "that it was *my* tech that failed and you're the one who saved the mission."

Liao's shoulders lower a little as she regards him.

Chase looks between the two of them, surprised.

"And I realized," Torbjörn continues, "that if anyone is going to judge you for the work you did in the past, they will have to judge me too. It's my work on the Titans that the omnics have weaponized—I designed that model myself, years ago. I saw them as simple algebra, an engineering puzzle that needed a solution, building something so large with those capabilities. The first time we succeeded on our prototype, I didn't know where they'd end up, I thought they'd just be used for building skyscrapers. I'd been considering a problem, a design challenge, and I was proud to answer it."

There's a heavy silence between them.

"Talking to Campbell after the report," Torbjörn says, "I guess I saw something I recognized in his distrust of you. Something I didn't like. And it made me realize that"—he takes a long, deep breath—"I owe you an apology."

Both Chase and the doctor exchange a look of surprise.

"This mission was a success, and . . . it would have gone very differently without you. I fear I may have, well, misjudged you, Mina. And I'm sorry for it."

"Thank you." Liao blushes a little, clearly pleased, but she seems to have the self-control to be gracious.

"We're a team, and as my wife reminds me, I don't always make teamwork easy."

"We can't change the past"—Liao looks between them—"no matter how desperately we may long to."

Both Chase and Torbjörn agree with her, a hidden regret in all their eyes.

"But we can look forward. And your kindness means a lot to me."

They shake hands, and Chase is heartened to see it. The conversation itself seems to have worn him out, though, and Torbjörn says only a few more words before leaving.

Chase and Liao turn to each other in surprise.

"Never thought I'd see the day." Liao laughs to herself and settles into her office chair, spinning lazily from side to side. "It's true, though," Liao says. "What he said about the unforeseen ends our creations come to. The omniums too were designed to meet a challenge—the soaring demand for robots that the corporation was struggling to meet."

Chase thinks for a moment about Torbjörn, standing on a platform of scaffolding, directing engineers constructing the Titans, or Liao putting the finishing touches on a prototype omnic in a clinical-looking lab. But with the advent of the omniums, the robots began building themselves . . . a reality they're all suffering under now. Chase remembers Omnica Corporation's promotional videos, showing the factory building omnics all on its own. Massive metal arms installing various parts. Glossy machines sliding off assembly lines with a frightening, clockwork efficiency.

"They were shut down, though," Chase says. "For years. Do you ever think about why or how they came back online?"

"All the time," Liao muses. "That's one of the mysteries of the Crisis. If we knew that, we'd be closer to understanding why this all happened. And then maybe we'd have a chance to undo it."

"You know," Chase says, "early on in the Crisis I kept studying the way that the omnics attacked the cities, to see if I could notice any patterns."

Chase logs into Liao's terminal, makes a couple of hand motions, and the display on one of the large monitors changes. It resolves into a familiar map: Lagos at the start of the Crisis. With arrows and darts to indicate the pattern of attack.

"I started to talk to Jack about it," Chase says. "You can overlay the attack on Mexico City or Hong Kong, any of those cities first hit hard, and the omnics use the same strategies. But as you fast forward, you can pinpoint where humanity starts to change the game."

She gestures to a huge loss of omnic units. "This—Egypt deployed their elite sniper team for the first time here. It was all over the base how they'd won big. CSOR was preparing our own sniper teams for major field ops—but it only took a week and then…"

The screen changes, with omnics deploying fast and fighting up close. "They changed tactics at the same moment. Not just in Egypt—it happened everywhere."

"I've never studied their attack patterns like this," Liao says, squinting at the screens. "Machine learning is advanced, but the data the omnics were receiving was unique. I would assume different nations' armies had different responses, different weaponry. Even the terrain the omnics had to overcome and the layout of the cities—"

"So how did they do it?" Chase wonders. "It's too many variables for them to all make the same assumptions and the same changes to their strategy. Their formations and timings were the exact same."

"The patterns of dispersion, the fighting, but also the type and number of units produced by the omniums . . . fascinating. Like they accounted for every variable from every nation's fight and arrived at a strategy that outwitted them all."

Chase switches to another screen, again showing the same result. "Could they all be communicating? Are they capable of that?"

"Across the globe? Instantaneously?" Liao frowns a little. "There are millions and millions of units—communication among all of them would be chaos. At least, not without some sort of hierarchy to filter all the information, come up with a winning course of action, and direct the units appropriately."

"So . . . a puppeteer. A single outside source taking in all the data and spitting out orders," Chase suggests. "Is that possible?"

"No," Liao says resolutely.

Silence stretches between them.

Of course it wouldn't be that easy, Chase thinks. *If it were, humanity would've figured this out by now.*

"Well," Liao begins, "I wouldn't know where to even begin

to disprove that theory with an omnic, but the omniums utilized our eleventh-generation XH1F telecommunications system. It was designed to share data between omniums for supply-chain management, resource sharing, software upgrades. If someone external was controlling the *omnium*, they would have to use that system to deliver the kind of immediate orders we've seen."

"In theory," Chase says. She wants it to be true. This fight could be so much simpler if it were true.

"I suppose I could"—the doctor starts typing something quickly into her data pad—"see if I can find information on the network traffic. There shouldn't be any, but if there is . . ."

Chase is quiet for a little while, her mind whirring as she considers the implications of what they're discussing.

"Oh!" The doctor points to a display.

"I'm not sure what I'm looking at," Chase admits.

"This graph shows that there is a lot of activity on the network," Liao says. "Which means—at least, it's compelling evidence that the theory . . . could be true."

"So, could we . . . ?" Chase begins, but then shakes her head, as if the notion is too far-fetched.

"What?" Liao pushes.

"Well, if the omniums are receiving orders from some outside source . . . could we cut them off? It wouldn't do much to stop the omnics that are already out there, but if the Detroit omnium stopped making new units . . ."

Liao's eyes widen.

Whenever Chase considers the war as a game they're playing,

she thinks of the omnics as pawns and the omnium—deadly and impenetrable—as the king.

"It would give us the kind of opening we need to turn the tide."

The idea is outrageous, would have seemed completely impossible to her before. But something about their success today has renewed her faith in the fight.

She poses it as a hypothetical over dinner, standing with Liao at the head of the table, its sides lined by the engineering team—who always seem to eat together—along with Torbjörn and Jack. Sergeant Grayson and a few of the younger detachment members are in the middle of a heated debate about what is the most-sided object it's possible to tessellate. Chase is happy to interrupt them before their philosophical debate turns into a food fight.

"In a theoretical world," Chase says, a little breathless, "how would one destroy an omnium?"

A surprised silence falls across them. In the bright fluorescent lights, they all look exhausted. Chase has been thinking about what it would mean if they could take out the omnium, if they could arrive at this tipping point that could help them win the war. It may even be the only way to win. With the Detroit omnium sending out soldiers every day, it's only a matter of time before every city is completely overwhelmed. But if they take it out of commission, Canada could have a fighting chance.

Jack ventures, "Several tons of hypothetical explosives?"

Liao shakes her head. "The omnium has a nuclear fusion core, remember? This isn't just a matter of fallout—the resulting explosion could literally destroy the planet."

Jack gives it another go. "Could we set up the Siege around it and destroy any omnics that come out?"

Torbjörn shakes his head. "The omnium is the size of a small city in its own right, and surrounded by antiaircraft weaponry that's too advanced for us to overcome. We would need to install the Siege at multiple points around the omnium, and then have back-up turrets ready to reinforce our position as we lose units. I don't think we have enough firepower... even if we had the full might of Overwatch and the CAF."

"And we can't cut off its power source, since it's self-sustaining," Jack says.

Liao nods.

"Are there other resources the omnium is reliant on?" Jack asks. "Titanium? Silicone? Microchips?"

"Starving the omnium and surrounding region of those resources could be a decades-long effort," Grayson jumps in. "We don't have that kind of time."

They all lapse into a miserable silence. Grayson and Jack pick at their chili. The chatter of the other soldiers in the mess hall echoes around them. Two tables down, a group is singing "Happy Birthday."

Liao finally breaks the silence. "Chase and I have actually been thinking that the omnium could be... being controlled. From outside."

"Is that likely?" Jack asks.

"More likely than we initially thought," Chase adds.

Liao pulls up the graph on her data pad. "There's a telecommunications system that should be dead, but the network traffic shows it's online and relaying orders."

The two of them explain their theory again to the group, who listen intently.

"So, what are you suggesting?" Jack asks. "Interrupt the signal somehow?"

"Sort of," Liao says. "We don't necessarily need to destroy the omnium if we can cut it off from the outside world. We would have to go inside to do it, though. There are five internal access points that would need to be physically disconnected in order to quarantine the omnium from outside control . . . if that's what's really happening."

"Getting inside would be next to impossible, though." Torbjörn sounds wary, and Chase also shudders at the thought. It's the belly of the beast. Hard to imagine going in and ever coming out again. "And even then, none of us have ever seen the inside of an omnium, or these access points—"

"I have," Liao says.

"No," Jack interjects.

Grayson cocks an eyebrow. "I thought this was hypothetical."

"Field ops were never part of her job description," Jack says.

Liao leans forward. "I can do it."

"That's not the problem. You're too valuable to risk, and you don't have the training. You can talk us through this on the comms, from the base."

"There's no way the omnics don't have a signal jammer in place around the omnium. Once you're in range of it, I guarantee you, comms will be useless."

"Then draw us a map, show us how to disable these—"

"A *map*?" she says, incredulous. "That omnium is the size of a small *city*. And none of you are familiar with Omnica's tech. You'll never make it to the access points."

"It would be dangerous," Torbjörn adds. "Maybe a one-way mission. Especially if you're wrong. And even if you're not, disabling the omnium won't stop the omnics. It will only stop the omnium from making *more*. There's a good chance we could be overwhelmed . . . and the omnics could just march back inside and repair what we destroyed."

Liao isn't backing down. "I want to stop this Crisis . . . to do everything I can. This is something I can do."

"Okay," Chase cuts in. She nods at Liao, then stands up. "So . . . can we do this? Is it possible?"

"We'll need all the firepower we can get," Torbjörn says. "In the air and on the ground. There'll be more Titans and Bastions; we'll need to be able to counter. Tanks, I'd suggest, and more troops, from the CAF and Overwatch."

Jack nods. "The US military will have to be on board, of course, since it's in their territory. I could make some calls—I think they would be open to it. They might even provide us with some resources, but they have their hands full too. It will be a massive battle just getting to the front door."

"The bigger challenge might be getting command on board . . . ," Chase says.

"And this goes nowhere if all three organizations don't sign off on this mission," Jack finishes.

But in spite of the hurdles, there is an excitement among the group, a new energy. Hope and fear. Can they do this?

They're willing to die trying.

6

LAURENTIDES

What would it be like, waking up in another body? Faster reflexes, keener hearing, strength, more efficient everything. Chase longs for it. Is excited about the idea of meeting her new self.

Chase stays up until the early hours of the morning with Jack, Liao, and the engineers, planning their mission proposal in detail. They carefully study everything they can find from the archived files that Liao manages to source from her days at Omnica Corp. They contain manuals and schematics, detailed layouts of the Outback omnium in Australia, where she was stationed. It isn't the same as Detroit, but they all follow the same core functionality and use the same tech.

Chase uses the resources to devise strategies, troop formations, and numbers. Who goes where? How long will they have to execute this plan? It's a delicious challenge for her tactical mind. And afterward, as they're all heading to bed, she finds a new resolve in herself.

"If we run the omnium op in two weeks, is that enough time… to do what we discussed?"

"What?" the doctor asks, running a hand through her jet-black hair. She looks tired out by all the work they've been doing, and it takes her a moment to grasp what Chase is referring to.

"The upgrades to my cybernetics," Chase says, and the doctor musters a sleepy smile.

"Oh!"

Working with Liao, Chase had come to trust the doctor, and—on some level—to understand her. But more than that, Chase had come to understand more about herself. She'd spent too long caught between loving her augmentations and her fear of being different. As a child, she often focused on the things her body held her back from. Sitting on the bench in school, those days as she was getting sicker, when she was unable to participate in sports or play with her friends at lunchtime. That feeling—loneliness mixed with some familiar shame at what made her different. The ways her body stopped her from doing the things she dreamed of doing.

But then, she reached the right age and had her first cybernetic procedure, reborn into a new body she thanked daily for all it gave her. And things only got better—with more and more soldiers relying on cybernetic enhancements for their recovery, pressure increased for the CAF to change their guidelines for military fitness. At age sixteen, Chase was allowed to enlist in the primary reserves, and she easily met all the fitness standards. Her cybernetics could be kept in working order when they broke; she could get another procedure when she needed treatment for her illness. There were always those like Campbell who believed her inferior, but their opinions seldom mattered when, over every deployment, she could prove them wrong.

That all seemed to change when the Crisis hit, and with every mission she'd begun to feel as if her cybernetics weighed her down. The scrapes and dings on her prostheses were hard to look at day after day. Not being able to source the hydraulic fluid for her leg had slowed her down for a couple of weeks, and the base doctor had been very little help. The new environment brought back all those vulnerabilities she'd once felt about her body. It made her even more on edge to know that, all the while, command was scrutinizing her performance, waiting to see if she would fail.

The past few missions have changed her. Chase's mind keeps drawing her back to the conversation she had with Jack in Davenport House. Not a day goes by when she doesn't think about Helena or Bonnie or the team members that she lost. Her augmentations allowed her to see the danger coming, true, but she is done feeling hopeless, able to do nothing more than warn her troops before an evacuation. Her cybernetics make her stronger, faster—they can make a difference in battle—most importantly, they are part of her, and Chase is tired of hiding who she is.

Chase smiles. "How soon can you do it?"

"I'll have to source a few things, and reserve time with Dr. Hendon, but . . . early next week?"

"I'm set to run point on a short mission then, setting up the Siege on a couple of major highways."

"Jack and the others might get along without you for that one," Liao says, "if Major Campbell can sign you off. You'll need a day to recover, and some time to acclimate to the changes."

"I'll try." In her excitement, Chase hadn't factored recovery time into this.

"But," Liao says, "if the commanding officer gives us permission to attack the Detroit omnium, we'll all be grateful for your upgraded cybernetics. I know I will. Our team will need every advantage it can get."

The nights of sleep deprivation finally take their toll on Chase. Once her head touches her pillow, she tumbles as heavily into sleep as a rock into a lake.

A drone's digital call wakes her what feels like seconds later. All through breakfast, nerves twist her stomach. Her team have devised a great plan and a strong argument to command, but how many times has she pitched what feels like a great plan only for Major Campbell and the other officers to reject it?

Later that morning, Chase and her team make their brilliant pitch, then wait in the brightly lit hall for the higher-ups to deliberate.

"Does this feel like it's taking longer than usual?" Liao asks.

Jack nods, anxious too.

Torbjörn is pacing up and down the hall, his boots making the ground shudder.

Grayson and the engineers are deep in discussion about nuclear fusion.

Finally, they're called back in.

"We've reached a decision," says Commanding Officer Fournier. She's seated on the other end of the varnished table next to Major Campbell and three others. The faces of a dozen people who are connected via video conferencing flicker on the surrounding monitors. Chase is reminded of the thesis she once did at university.

"The panel has approved your mission." There is an almost audible sigh of relief in the room. "But Major Campbell has made a convincing case for a change in personnel."

His cheeks and nose look slightly sunburned—probably from the glare off the snow outside—his skin peeling a little, like glue. He stands and, looking Chase in the eyes, says, "We are recommending that Captain Vivian Chase be placed on immediate leave."

The words are like a punch in the stomach. Chase feels all the blood drain from her face, clammy sweat pricking her palms. *What?* is the only word she can manage to mumble. Along with Jack, who shouts, and Torbjörn, who swears under his breath.

"You've not been in top form lately," Campbell says. He begins ticking off offenses on his fingers. "The failures in the Montréal rescue mission—"

"She saved more than one hundred people," Liao interrupts, abandoning any attempt at military protocol.

"The failure in Ottawa—"

"That was not her fault," Jack cuts in now. "And if it wasn't for Captain Chase, more people would have died."

"The retreat in Old Toronto—"

"That mission was a success!" Torbjörn says.

"If losing a third of your troops was how the CAF judged success, we would've lost this fight long ago."

Chase feels winded, dizzy, hard to articulate how completely unfair this feels. *He might as well blame me for the bad weather.*

"A good captain accounts for everything," Campbell says. "It has not escaped our attention that this string of losses began during the Crisis and was exacerbated after Dr. Liao upgraded your cybernetic eyes."

"My work has nothing to do with this," Liao says.

"Nothing?" Campbell raises his head in challenge. "You expect me—us—to believe that the mastermind of Omnica Corp's final era had nothing at all to do with this?"

"Are you suggesting that Dr. Liao is sabotaging us?" Jack says, stepping forward defensively.

"She's risking her life to help us," Torbjörn says now. "And what should Chase have done after that dogfight in Montréal? Shoot with a busted eye? You're suggesting medical attention is—"

"I'm *suggesting*," Major Campbell says slowly, "that Chase's cybernetics are a security risk we should have considered before. She is basically part omnic—"

"There it is," Chase finally says.

"This is ludicrous," Liao cries. "The upgrades I provided and would ever provide are completely compatible with Overwatch's guidelines. If necessary, I can submit a thorough report about the specifics."

"So this is an official order? She's barred from the mission?" Jack asks.

"Effective tomorrow at twelve hundred hours," Commanding Officer Fournier says, not meeting Chase's eyes, "Captain Vivian Chase is placed on mandatory leave, pending further review."

It all happens so fast. The next thing Chase knows, she is walking up the sun-bleached corridor outside the strategy room and into the melting snow. The cold seldom burns anymore, but this time something does.

She lets the brisk air fill her lungs, which are vise-tight with tension. She feels sick. The gut-churning mix of rage and despair that would have sent her crying to her bedroom when she was younger. But she's a captain now, a troop commander, doing the job she's always wanted to do. Jack comes running out after her. "Hey," he shouts but she's still walking quickly away and he must run to catch up with her.

"Captain! Chase," he says, but now it hurts to hear it. "They're wrong about you." Then, touching her shoulder to make her stop walking. "They'll come to their senses."

"They won't," Chase says without turning.

"It was the same with me at first. There were people who thought that Overwatch shouldn't accept—"

"It's not the same, though," Chase interrupts. "*We're* not. You *chose* this. Risked your life for it. My cybernetics saved my life.

I love them for that. But I've always known that there are people in the military who think they make me weak—a liability. So, for years, I've done everything I can to hide my differences, I'm careful not to talk about them and to never to ask for special treatment.

"But, just when I decide that I'm done apologizing for who I am, just as I'm letting myself embrace my differences, I discover that, to them, my differences are worse than a weakness—they make me a *traitor*."

Jack flinches at the word, horrified too. "We're going to fight this. We can—"

"Maybe I'm done fighting." Chase takes a deep breath, the cold burning her throat. "If command doesn't see my value, I'll have to find another way to do what I'm called to do."

"It'll be their loss," Jack agrees. A little icon in the corner of Chase's vision tells her she's late for a training session. She's meant to lead several of her detachment leaders in a VR fight against a Titan. She's determined to see her people one last time, to do this one last thing to prepare them, before she maybe never sees them again.

Chase grits her teeth and shakes it off. Then heads in for the fight.

Combat is never as frightening in virtual reality. Although her VR visor renders the size of the warbot in true scale, nothing can mimic the way the air shifts around it. The shudder in the ground it creates, like a shifting of the earth's tectonic plates.

This time, they're in an abandoned mall when four Titans rip through the building's central concourse. It's down to Chase and a couple of her detachment leaders to tackle it. In the simulation her gun doesn't seem to work quite the same way. It takes longer to recharge, and her aim isn't as accurate. But still, it takes her and the other soldiers about forty minutes to disable and destroy all four omnics. It requires almost all their firepower and teamwork.

Chase is about to deal the killing shot to the final Titan when it comes back to her with crushing clarity: she won't be there for their next mission. With a twist of guilt and regret in her stomach, she realizes that she has to let them go, watch them succeed without her. She steps back, and the Titan takes a lazy swing at her. It is Noah who leaps up the frozen escalator to the fifth-floor balcony of the mall and fires his gun into the Titan's head. With a satisfying burst of electronics, its central processing unit explodes.

Chase remembers when these simulations used to make her feel good, ready for anything. Today she feels deflated, spent.

Her troops all cheer and laugh, though. They high-five among the building-size carcasses of the robots before it all fades into nothing. The black grid lines on a white background indicate to Chase that the game is over.

With it, there's a sinking in her chest as she grapples around for the right words to give her squadron.

"Well done, team," she says, cheeks still flushed with pride, although she must work hard to keep some lightness in her voice.

Noah turns to her, and Chase has to fight the urge to look away. They haven't spoken since the day they lost Helena. Some part of her is worried that he'll never speak to her again.

Now is the time, though. Chase isn't sure if they've heard the news, if the base's gossip mill could churn out the rumors that quickly, but she knows they have to hear it from her, regardless.

"As I'm sure you've already heard," she says, out of some impulse to get ahead of it while she still can, "I'm being placed on immediate leave."

She notices that the detachment leaders already seem distracted. They're whispering amongst themselves, then looking up at the glass-fronted viewing gallery a floor above, where a couple of shadows are flitting. Someone curses under his breath.

Chase wonders if she is about to be disciplined for continuing with this training session instead of waiting in her bunk for further instruction.

"I wanted more than anything to be with you all in Detroit—" She must fight, then, against a catch in her throat.

"Permission to speak, sir," Noah says, putting down his VR gun. Chase is about to reply—wondering why he is choosing to be so formal—when she realizes that he's staring up at the viewing gallery.

At Major Campbell, who presses the intercom and says, "Great practice. Well done."

"Major Campbell, sir." Noah raises his voice so that he can be heard better. "If Chase has been taken off the mission, I will not be reporting for duty."

Chase feels emotion welling up inside her. She knows what this means for him to take a stand on her behalf like this, especially after what happened in Toronto.

"Stand down, Sergeant" is all she can muster. She can't meet Noah's eye for fear that she will lose her usually firm grip on her emotions.

"Well, son," Campbell says, the tightness in his lips only wavering a little, "that would be desertion. I'm not sure you're prepared for those consequences—"

"Me too," says a shadow behind Major Campbell in the viewing gallery. It's Sergeant Mason, who—as he is still recovering from his injuries—Chase isn't sure is even cleared for the mission. But the sentiment is kind anyway.

"Well—" Campbell sounds as if he's about to belabor this point when Sergeant Harper puts down his VR gun too.

"I will not be reporting for duty either, sir."

"Me too," says Avery.

"And me," says Jake.

"Or me," says Camille.

"Don't do this," Chase says, low. "It isn't worth it."

"Interesting to see what kind of insubordination Captain Chase has allowed to flourish in her ranks," Campbell says, staring down his nose at them.

What can he do, though? Chase wonders as more cries of support ring out. This is half of CSOR. Even if they're disciplined, the mission will be impossible to complete without any detachment leaders or their captain.

Noah continues, "Captain Chase is the best of us, sir. A good mentor to me, a kind friend. Around the bunk, they call her *Sojourn.*"

Chase finally meets his gaze, comes close to crumbling.

"Because she'll go wherever she has to, risk whatever she needs to, to save lives . . ." Noah takes a deep breath. "And to bring back as many of her soldiers as possible.

"Sergeant Helena Dean was one of the many we lost in Toronto. She is—was"—a shudder of pain from him at the word, a breath through gritted teeth—"very special to me. I know that Chase did her best, through that mission and all the others. Planning the evacuations, waiting until the last person was on the stratoscopter before jumping in herself. And saving my life too. I wouldn't be standing here if it wasn't for her."

"You'd really follow her into battle," Campbell asks, "knowing that her cybernetics could risk the whole platoon? Could be the reason Sergeant Dean died?"

"That can't be true," Sergeant Mason says from the gallery. "Her cybernetics helped saved my life."

"She saved all of us," says Camille. "She saw the Detonator before anyone else."

"And the Titan," Mason says.

"She's up every night in the strategy room."

"She never stops!"

"Yes, but can you trust her?" Campbell says.

"With our lives, sir!" they all shout back.

It's only then that Chase notices the chill on the back of her neck as the door to the practice room slides open. In the light that pours in, Chase sees about thirty shadows fall across the ground. There seem to be more figures up in the viewing gallery now as well, curious to watch the standoff, she supposes.

"We trust her too." It's Torbjörn who steps forward into the middle of the practice room, the Overwatch troops behind him. Chase can see Jack and Dr. Liao among the rest of her soldiers as well.

Campbell cuts a lonely figure all of a sudden, at one end of the viewing gallery.

"Captain Vivian Chase is vital to the success of our mission," Jack says. "And if the CAF has no interest in deploying her, Overwatch command has agreed to welcome her into our forces . . . if she'll join us."

Chase is speechless, a little light-headed at this change of events.

"All right," comes Commanding Officer Fournier's voice from one end of the viewing gallery. "This is all quite enough."

At first, Chase thinks these words are directed at the crowd assembled in the practice room, but then Chase realizes that the commanding officer is looking at Campbell.

"I've had the chance to review some of the notes Dr. Liao kindly sent me, and I have to agree that the suspicions about Chase's cybernetics are unfounded.

"Captain Vivian Chase"—she turns now to the window— "I am relieved to say that the recommendation for your dismissal has been rejected. You are returned to active duty, effective immediately. Make us proud."

DETROIT

Chase remembers being fifteen, sitting next to her father and watching as two tennis players competed for the championship at Wimbledon. *Magic* had been the word he'd used, and it had filled her with such hopeless longing. Because he had been right. Magic, everything from the soles of their feet to their calves and hands. At the end of their wrists, the electric-lime ball was magic and the turf under their soles, the way it all defied gravity.

Chase feels magic this crisp morning, as she sprints to the summit of the mountain. Magic, everything: the sunrise glancing off the dew-wet spines of branches, and the melting snow, the newly flowering green buds unfurling everywhere, the ground under her heels, her lungs and spine, the pneumatic cylinders in her calves, the way that she too can seem to defy gravity.

It's been two days since the upgrades, and this morning

Chase chose to go for a run on the mountain just for the thrill of it. Her nerves are wound tight. Today is the day that they storm the omnium. She works hard to stop her mind from considering all the possibilities, everything that could go wrong, all the ways this mission could end in disaster. But the run helps. Keeps her centered in her body and the world around her.

It feels as if spring is nearly here. More hardy tufts of grass are poking through the melting frost, snowdrop flowers are rearing their delicate heads. Spiders spin webs between boughs, ice suspended like crystals on their silk. Chase feels like part of it somehow on her faster, stronger legs. At one with it.

She's dashing up a narrow passage, cobbles sliding under her heels, when she senses a shift in the air. Something nearby. Her new reflexes kick in, this function her legs can do now—a duck and slide. She falls to the ground and activates her calf and knee booster, which creates a forward motion when she touches the ground.

"Nice move." It's Jack's unmistakable voice from behind her.

"Thanks. It's new." Chase smiles and keeps running.

It turns into a lighthearted race; the two of them bounding up the mountain pass, over scraggy cliffs, in and out of lichen-striped trees. The sound of their feet startles wild rabbits and makes birds erupt from the trees, scattering shards of frost in their wake.

Chase and Jack reach the pinnacle of the mountain winded and laughing, their breath coming out in white plumes. The view from here is magnificent. The mountains and the lakes. Snowmelt sluicing over rocks and into ravines. The trees and underbrush, the sharp cry of hunting animals. The sun is higher in the sky, bright marigold light on the horizon. It feels . . . wild here. Like nature fighting back. Like she could forget all about the war. All about the robots and the fallen cities and the challenge ahead of them. Sometimes, she wants to.

"I think we can agree that was a draw," Jack says, still breathing heavily.

"Of course." Chase smirks. "If by 'draw' you mean that I won." They both laugh, and it feels good. Every waking hour has been focused on their preparations for the upcoming mission. Over the last few days they've been memorizing maps, simulating the inside of the omnium in the VR room during training. Liaising with the US military, who have agreed to support the route with airstrikes and even provided tanks. No amount of preparation, though, will untangle the knot of nerves in her stomach.

Chase wonders if their thoughts have wandered in the same direction, because their laughter fades quickly into a contemplative silence.

Although Chase understands that the risks are high, there's nowhere else she'd rather be than fighting with her team.

"Thank you." She realizes now that she hasn't said it to Jack before. "Thanks for fighting for me to stay on the team."

"Well"—Jack laughs—"it wasn't entirely selfless—I knew that without you we wouldn't have a fighting chance."

Chase shades her eyes against the rising sun. "I wish it didn't bother me," she says more quietly. "Campbell, the other officers, the people who think that augmented soldiers have no place in the CAF."

"You'll get there," Jack says, staring in the same direction. "I did."

"Yeah?"

Chase remembers reading about the Soldier Enhancement Program. She heard that it was met by a wave of opposition. Riots broke out near Washington, even in the face of the Crisis; some people were horrified by the genetic engineering taking place in the laboratories. There were heated debates and think pieces. People wondering whether creating augmented soldiers would fundamentally alter what it meant to be human. Chase wondered for a while about it.

"Did that . . . ever bother you? The things they said about people like you?"

Jack seems calm, like he's somewhere else on his journey. "No. But like you said, it was different for me and Gabe—we chose this. You didn't." He takes a deep breath. "But the way I see it . . . human, transhuman, cybernetic, augmented, enhanced—it's not what your heart is made of that matters. It's what you do with it. Who you defend, what you choose to live for that matters."

His words remind her: "I got some good news yesterday."

"Oh yeah?" he says. "I could do with some good news."

"My niece." Chase has only distantly alluded to Bonnie before, but she explains now. "She was hurt pretty badly on the first day of the Crisis. She's been in the hospital for a long time now. She was attacked, nearly drowned. They thought she might never walk again, but some doctor has been suggesting cybernetics could help her."

"Just like you," Jack finishes.

"They're my thing," Chase says. "Bonnie and my sister. My family. They're who I'll always fight for. Someday soon . . . I'm going to bring them home."

It's a long journey on the stratoscopter. When they finally cross the border and Chase catches sight of the omnium on the horizon, she feels a chill creep into her blood. The automated factory is on the outskirts of Detroit, near the township of Sumpter. Seeing it from here, Chase is reminded of driving to theme parks—how she could see the huge rides on the horizon from far away. How the sight of the drop tower and the pendulum rides or the apex of the biggest roller coaster would make her believe she was almost there, then she'd be disappointed to discover that they still had a half hour or more to drive. The omnium is much the same—a city-size factory many stories high, spread across several square kilometers. The size of it tricks her into thinking that they are closer than they are.

Below them, Detroit looks postapocalyptic, has been decimated by the omnics, entire swaths of it on fire, belching gouts of flame into the overcast sky.

All omniums are slightly different. This one bears the familiar trapezoidal shape, but has parts that look completely foreign, like something built by giant bees or termites. It has a kind of alien symmetry, with several domes that consist of hundreds of thousands of geodesic discs. When this one was built, it was considered an architectural marvel, with tubular steel frames and hexagonal external cladding panels made of a lightweight but diamond-hard metal alloy. The sight of it has always reminded Chase a little of the Montréal Biosphere, an environmental museum on Saint Helen's Island she once visited that was designed by Buckminster Fuller.

The stratoscopter drops them eighty kilometers from the omnium, where they meet with Captain Page from the US Army. He and Jack greet each other warmly; apparently they know each other. Captain Page commands a company of five platoons, with air and ground cavalry units.

As they expected, the omnium is surrounded by warbots. As soon as Captain Page gives the all clear, the combined air forces begin pelting the omnium with the airstrikes. The attack succeeds in thinning out the ground units and provides enough time for Torbjörn and the engineer sergeants to set up the Siege on the edge of the battlefield. Chase and her team watch as the omnium's antiaircraft system launches a counteroffensive.

This is all part of the plan that Chase devised. She hoped that the US battle tanks, her CAF troops combined with Overwatch, and an operational Siege system would lend them enough firepower to engage the omnics in a massive ground battle. It's looking good so far. Chase smiles as she watches the herons take to the sky and the turrets charge into the battle. Her detachments will fight their way into the omnium, and then she will dispatch them in groups led by Dr. Liao and the engineer sergeants to disconnect each port and quarantine the omnium from outside control.

With the turrets operational, Chase and her team now ride in, ready for the fight. The US Army's battle tanks combined with the turrets are well matched against the Huntsmen and Bastions. Chase commanded the tanks to spearhead the assault. She and her detachment follow after in armored fighting vehicles.

"How are they doing?" Liao asks Chase over the comms. It's strange to see her here, in the same kind of uniform as Jack and Torbjörn, head almost totally obscured by her helmet and visor.

Chase overlays a map onto her vision so she can see the troop movements. "Going to plan," she tells the doctor. The best they can hope for. On the map, Chase watches as an Overwatch squad charges at a fleet of Huntsmen and manages to disable them, the heavy machines splashing into the mud.

"Move out!" Chase gives the order to her soldiers, and they all jump out, ready to charge at the enemy and fight their way into the omnium. Chase and her detachment launch themselves at a phalanx of Bastions led by an OR14, attacking the warbots from all directions—hurling grenades and firing, coming up against their enemy like waves against a cliff face. The Bastions reconfigure into tank mode and fire back in retaliation, tearing holes in the ground and sending half of them scattering. A shadow flashes across the mud. Without looking up, the smart display on Chase's eyes tells her that there is a heron above. It spies the danger the troops are in and, moments later, redirects a turret aiming to fire at the Bastions. Explosions that they all take cover from. Shocking to watch, the projectiles striking the omnics like a bolt of lightning.

Another glance at her smart display tells her that only one of her detachment members has been injured, and he's being taken to the medevac van.

Turning back to the omnium, Chase can hardly believe it. The field is clearing, the enemy forces thinning. She sees an opening now, a path through the wreckage of warbots that will give them access to the omnium.

"This way!" she shouts, leading the charge. The entrance is still about two kilometers away, but Chase's keen eyes spy the route to the access hatch Liao highlighted for her back at the base, a human entrance usually used for maintenance, one that is likely unguarded by the omnics.

And with their rapidly decreasing numbers, Chase believes it: The omnics seem to be pushing themselves out too far, leaving their squadrons exposed on all sides to attack, the omnium undefended. Chase can't help but rush toward it, her cybernetic legs practically flying over the mud. Her soldiers are behind her, Overwatch and the armored vehicles farther back. As Chase runs, she sees Jack too, darting and weaving across the battlefield, rifle ready to defend their combined forces.

The fight is going as well as she planned, Chase thinks with a distant flutter of pride. Maybe *better* than she planned, a thought that causes her to hesitate. Chase thinks back to her hospital room, to Shah Matt with her grandfather's old VAC caretaker omnic. How it moved as she moved. Even her best plans failed to shatter its defenses to take a pawn. But this—the omnium— was the omnics' king.

And what did the last battles teach her?

"There is always something else," she says to herself. Her visual feed tells her that Jack and the doctor are close by. They all watch in surprise as, at that moment, the omnium's sealed doors roll open. For a second, before Chase holds up her gun to fire, she thinks she can hear everyone catch their breath. The doors are many stories high, and the sound of them peeling open causes the ground to tremble. Into the bright light emerge a fleet of robots none of them have ever seen before. Ground units with armor like mackerel scales, cannons mounted on their shoulders and arms, feet the size of cars—a new evolution of the Titan.

"No," Chase says with a shallow gasp, but then the breath is knocked from her chest as something hits the side of her body and sends her flying. Chase opens her eyes and finds herself on her knees in the mud, Noah in front of her. Where she was standing is now a smoking hole in the ground; the new warbots opened fire. "You saved me," she barely has the time to tell him before she must leap to her feet and flee from the path of another missile.

All around her now, this new kind of rocket is striking the ground like a meteor shower. Chase and Noah race from the path of the warbots, who are fanning out from the open omnium. Although her troops are hurtling into the fight, they are horribly outmatched and—Chase can now see—overextended. The omnics sent out their smaller units to lure them in, to a distance beyond any hope of a speedy retreat.

And these new Titan units . . . even the tanks seem small in the shadow of the warbots. One of them stomps on an armored vehicle and crushes it like a milk carton. On her right, two tanks have been hit; she watches as they explode into flames.

"This way," Noah shouts, and the two of them take cover behind a stationary truck, breathing hard as the sounds of the battle rage around them.

"Chase," Jack says over the comms. "With these Titan units and the enemy reinforcements, we won't be able to make it to the access hatch. But there's a way in while the omnium is still open."

She looks up—at the massive holding bays the Titans came out of.

"It's not possible," Chase replies. "None of us will even make it to the front—we've already gone too far." A rocket explodes within range of them. She and Noah duck to save themselves from the damage, but splinters of white-hot metal still split the skin on her flailing arms

"Dr. Liao says she can program the herons to carry us in," Jack says.

Chase glances up at them, wheeling against the smoke-shrouded sky. Not one of them has been shot down—a variable the omnics still haven't been able to outwit. Carried by the herons, they will be invisible to the omnics, which should give them enough time to slide into the open door of the omnium.

"They can't carry us all though," Chase says, thinking about the numbers in her detachment. She'd planned for no less than twenty-five people to execute the mission inside the omnium—with teams of four covering each engineer. They can't lose that many herons from the field; it will decimate the effectiveness of the Siege.

Noah leans over the side of the vehicle and takes out a couple of Huntsmen heading their way.

"Probably only three of us can make it," Jack admits. "We might have a chance if you join me and Dr. Liao."

"No." Chase's heart sinks as she glances around at the devastation. The evolved Titans are tearing through her troops, their enormous feet churning the ground into muddy trenches that the tanks must swerve to avoid. Chase can't abandon her soldiers now—not in the face of such mounting loss. And how can she, Jack, and Liao disarm the omnium alone? The distance between the ports is massive, and if they encounter resistance inside . . . they won't get the job done quickly enough.

"This could be our only chance to get in, to prove the theory," Jack says. "We need to do it while the door is open. Dr. Liao is summoning the herons now."

"I can't leave my people behind," Chase says more quietly.

"The only way you can hope to save them is in there. If we don't act, we're all going to be overwhelmed by the omnics within the hour. Our troops have their mission," Jack says as a heron soars down and swoops at her. "We have ours."

The heron's rotor blades whip up the air like a cyclone. It's almost frightening, seeing one up close. They're much larger than they look from the ground, more like a dragon than a bird. A predator, and she's a darting minnow. Chase scans its body for a place to grip.

"Go!" Noah shouts at her, and running to grab the drone, she does.

The flight is terrifying. The heron's body rockets swiftly through the air, and Chase works hard to hang on. The ground drops away below her boots, and her stomach feels as if it has fallen into her knees. There is the battlefield below, splayed like a black-and-white chess board. Soldiers in scattering formations, like pieces, warbots bowling through them. Smoke everywhere, mud and gunfire. Blood crashing in her ears at the sight of it all.

When Chase looks up, she sees that she's been joined by Liao and Jack, who are also clinging to herons, winging their way toward the rapidly closing doors of the omnium. They are a few feet ahead of her, and as their herons bring them to the ground, Chase realizes that if she is going to make it inside in time, she's going to have to jump.

She's about fifty feet off the ground, upward of four stories, which Chase knows is the average lethal distance for a fall.

"Hurry!" Liao shouts into her comms.

Chase squeezes her eyes shut, and—hoping against hope that her augmented body will be able to survive the fall—she jumps.

It's a sickening drop. Chase has experience parachuting from planes, dropping into war zones, but it's another thing to fall knowing there is nothing but her own legs to catch her. Chase tries to attain a stable position. As her body gets closer to terminal velocity, the wind howls in her ears.

Chase has been trained not to look directly at the ground as she approaches it, but it's hard not to stare down and imagine her body in a bloodied heap. Chase lands feetfirst, with her knees bent. The hydraulics in her upgraded legs absorb a lot of the impact, and the mud cushions her as she hits the ground.

Her body shaking all over, her meager breakfast tossed around in her gut, knees aching, clothes soaked in dirt. *Too close*, she thinks. *But okay*. She fights against the strong urge to retch in the mud.

The sound of the fight comes into focus, and when Chase looks up, the door of the omnium is almost closed. Running the final ten meters, she pushes her cybernetic legs as fast as they can go. It takes everything she has to leave her soldiers behind. Not to fight with them the way they fought for her, when Campbell wanted her off this mission. But she tries to remind herself that they trust her, and so she will need to trust them… or all their sacrifices will be for nothing.

Chase runs in the shadow of the newly evolved Titans as it hits her that, if they lose here, these new units will be headed for her home—to retake Toronto, to squash the Siege and decimate the unprepared CAF. She thinks of her sister, Valentine, of Bonnie regaining hope in the hospital, and resolves to seize this day, her sole chance to kill the king in this real-life game of Shah Matt.

Chase whips through the air like a speeding bullet, and by the time she reaches the omnium, the door has slid down with an opening that is barely a meter from the ground. It's heavy and moving so fast that if she tries to crawl through, it will come down like a guillotine on her spine.

So Chase ducks down and slides, the pistons in her leg propelling her across the ground and into the omnium a split second before the door slams shut.

Sealing them all inside.

8

THE OMNIUM

The battle vanishes, or at least, it feels that way. As soon as the door snaps shut, her comms cut off with a howl of static. Jack and Liao groan in pain too, casting off their earpieces. Her vision, bleached by the sunlight, renders everything in shadow at first, until her low-light vision adjusts to the gloom.

"Is it always so dark in here?" Jack whispers, turning on the light above his visor. Chase imagined that the place would be as noisy as any factory, the air filled with the crash and churn of metal, gears grinding together, compressors hissing, chains and rollers interlocking. Instead, it's quiet as a tomb. Everything modern and sleek, perfectly streamlined.

"The omnics don't need much ambient light," Liao clarifies.

Neither does Chase, and now that her vision has adjusted, she beholds the structure in awe. It's more like a cathedral than a factory. From the maps she's seen, it's a torus shape, with the nuclear reactor core running through its heart. It's possible to see the entire central structure from here, as the building has five floors, which are divided into ever-smaller mezzanine decks that spiral into one another like an orange peel. Jack lets out a low whistle. The place is enormous, supported all around by vaults, flying buttresses, and carbon-fiber columns that run from the top floor to the ground. The structure itself looks several times the size of the CAF's mountain base, and it makes her head spin to remember that this structure is just a small sliver of the omnium.

As Chase looks around, she gleans something of how the place works. Raw material rides in from pallets in neighboring sectors, is reworked into various parts by massive machines and shuttled down the line. The parts are borne along devices like sleds that seem to float on strips of metal to other stations, where robotic arms, automated lasers, scanners, and conveyor rails assemble the raw metal, silicone, microchips, and polymers into slick, flawless war machines. It would be awe-inspiring if it wasn't so frightening—the speed at which the factory performs its task. Uncanny almost, as mechanical rabbits whipped from hats.

"We called them 'maglifts,'" Liao says as one of the sleds whizzes past. "Magnetic, so they require less energy to propel. We used to use them around the lab as well. But . . . lots of things are different from what I'm used to."

"Because of the differences between Detroit and Australia?" Chase asks.

"No. The omnics have . . . *changed* this place. These adjustments weren't made by human hands. I suppose it makes sense, though. That whole floor over there, and that . . . the omnium's reorganized itself to build all these new warbots."

On this floor—hundreds of meters high—Titans are put together. They start like metal skeletons and march themselves to different stations, where arms the size of pickup trucks affix breastplates and calves, faces and helmets. At the other end, the completed Titans stand with their lights dimmed. Quiet giants. Are they waiting for the intruders to get closer before snapping to life, to snatch them up and grind their bones to salt?

"The omnium doesn't know that we're here yet," Liao says. "But as soon as we deactivate the access points, I imagine they will fight with everything they have to defend it."

In the simulations they practiced, after they fought their way into the omnium, the Overwatch team, supported by the US Army, would battle the omnics inside the factory as a distraction, while Chase, Jack, Liao, and the engineer sergeants split into detachments and destroyed each of the access ports. Being trapped in here alone makes her feel hopeless and exposed. Just the three of them, against thousands of omnics . . .

"Okay," Chase says, strategizing, "we get up to the first server room together, and Dr. Liao will run us through how to find the access port and disconnect it. Then we split up, and—"

"Is that a good idea?" Liao peers up from under her helmet, and Chase can see the concern in her eyes. This is her first active combat mission—something already difficult due to her limited training—and the change of plan is clearly frightening her. The thought of the doctor fighting against a wall of omnics is upsetting to Chase as well.

"Jack and I will try to draw the omnics' attention to give you an easier time," she says. "But we're already completely outnumbered. Splitting up will give us the best chance to get to each of the access ports as quickly as possible. Otherwise," as the engineers ominously mentioned during their concept-of-operations meeting...

"The omnium will find a way to reconnect itself," Liao finishes.

"So"—Jack nods—"disconnect the first one together. Then take out one each and reconvene on the final port before fighting our way out?"

"That's right," Chase says. The plan seems like a Hail Mary. She feels, with a kind of weary certainty, that they're not all going to make it. But she tries not to show it as the doctor points them in the direction of the first server.

"Maybe we should work backward," Jack suggests, "start with the server farthest away, and then we'll be close to the exit when we've completely disconnected the omnium?"

This sounds like as good a plan as any. The farthest server, though, is on the top floor, a dizzying height away, and when they arrive at the elevator, they find only an empty shaft.

"The omnium seems to have redesigned its interior to optimize means of production," Liao notes.

"The maglift!" Chase suggests as another rides like a bullet train past them.

"Good idea," Jack says, and they rush after it.

Chase gets there first, lunges for Liao's hand, and tosses her up onto the maglift. Then she throws her already-bruised body onto the flying magnetic sled. Jack lands next to her as the world whizzes by.

"Thank you," Liao says, her face red with the effort of the run. "Though, they come by every two minutes. We could have caught the next one."

Before she's finished speaking, they're already a floor up. Chase still feels a little dizzy from her heron jump and clings tightly to the vehicle. A lot of the rooms and areas they pass seem mysterious to her. Robot arms building batteries, or processors, unrecognizable machine parts. Sparks fly from welders, air hisses out of compressors. The sound of water gushes through pipes. Chase learned during a briefing that the entire factory relies on a sophisticated water-cooling system.

A couple more floors up and Chase feels as if they're scaling the CN Tower, but the distance gives her a good view of the layout of the place and which units are being assembled. On the lower floors are Titans, and a couple of giant omnics she's never seen before.

"The omnium must have invented them," Liao says, her face pale.

Frankenstein's monster, Chase thinks with a shudder, wondering what these machines will be like to fight. On some of the floors are more familiar enemies: Bastions, and Huntsmen, and on the top floors, OR14s are being molded and hammered together.

"Let's get off here," Liao instructs. They're far enough from the ground floor to trigger a nosebleed, and as they leap off the magnetic sled, Chase has to fight the twist of vertigo that comes over her when she looks down. In spite of the enormous size of the place, Chase can see most of the central structure.

"Come on." Jack nods in the direction of the server room, holding his gun up.

Although Chase follows suit, the sloping floors seem designed to disorient a human visitor.

"Careful not to touch anything," Liao says as they turn a corner into a long hall where OR14s are hooked to a railway on the ceiling. The partially assembled units are being wheeled along, a meter or so from the ground. It makes Chase feel as if she's in a forest of mechanical legs. Chase, Jack, and the doctor duck under floating feet, to the room that Liao highlighted in the layout. "I don't think they'll attack us until we actually do something to harm the omnium, but I can't rule it out either."

On the other side of the hall is the server room, a vast labyrinth of whirring machines that make a sound like waves breaking along the shore. Chase follows the doctor through the ordered server racks, flickering lights and coiled wires, routers and switches.

At the very far end of the room, buried amongst so much other machinery Chase would have had trouble identifying it herself, is the access point. It's a box the size of her palm, attached to the wall with two thick cables feeding into it. Liao told them it would not be enough to simply disconnect them; they would need to destroy them. She reaches into her tool belt and pulls out a laser cutter, slicing off the cables cleanly. For good measure, Chase bashes the box with the butt of her rifle. It takes a couple of hard smashes for the box to crack and spark, now useless.

"One down," Chase says, but they barely have enough time

to celebrate before the doors of the server room fly open and Huntsman units burst in. They leap over the racks, knocking wires and shelves over, their sensors flashing with cold violence.

Chase lifts her gun and fires at the oncoming Huntsmen. There are so many of them, though, leaping like lizards over the bodies of the others. One gets close enough to grab at Liao's collar. In its grip, she looks like a rag doll. It lifts her up and flings her across the room. Chase winces at the sound of her helmet cracking on a wall. Chase retaliates by shooting a couple of rounds into the warbot's head.

"Mina?" Jack shouts over the sound of glass and ceramic shattering, wires frying. He launches a helix rocket at the door. When it detonates, the explosion sends the omnics flying, and the room fills with smoke.

"Here . . . ," she splutters, picking herself up from the ground.

Chase looks around and notes, "They didn't fire their weapons at us."

"They're probably programmed to defend the omnium," Jack says. "If they fire inside the server room—"

"It could cause too much damage." Chase realizes that this may give them a small advantage.

The team manages to mow down enough robots to fight their way through the server room and back out the door, where they leap on top of an oncoming sled, the speed of it making air resistance whistle in their ears.

"There," Liao shouts at Jack, pointing down a hall that leads to the next server room. Chase is sure they would have flown past it if it wasn't for Liao.

"Good luck," Jack says as he leaps off the maglift and runs into a storm of omnic fire. Chase remembers the flash of his blue uniform as he vanishes and hopes it's not the last time she'll see him.

Almost too soon, her stop is approaching. "It'll be fine," Chase says, willing the words to be true. She puts on her best face, even as she's internally calculating how fast she can disable her access point and rendezvous on Liao's position for backup.

Liao smiles sadly. "To destroy the fifth access point, only one of us needs to make it."

"Right," says Chase as she leaves the doctor and rushes full pelt into the warbots. "You can do this."

And just like that, Chase is alone, pinned down under enemy fire, as Liao's figure is swallowed by the distance.

Chase must fight her way to the next access point. OR14s are leaping off the railings and bounding like leopards after her. On the battlefield, she's used to seeing OR14s as the lieutenants of an omnic squadron, but on this level the omnium is swarming with them.

With her new legs, Chase is fast enough to whip past most of them, firing at only the omnics in her way, ducking and sliding past the others. She can hear barely anything over the noise of grinding metallic joints and gears crunching as hundreds of omnics swing and grab for her.

The server room is in the same place as on the previous floor, though it's more difficult to find the access point without Liao's help.

Chase thinks she spots something that looks like the device Liao identified—it has the same matching wires, looks the same size. She is about to grab for it when a robot reaches her first. It takes hold of her shoulders and slams her to the floor.

Chase tastes blood in her mouth as her jaw clenches shut and the omnic comes at her again with its fist. She ducks, but another OR14 swings for her and crunches her rail gun under its heel. Chase could cry at the sight of it. But instead, she leaps to her feet and swings up onto one of the server racks.

From this vantage she is almost eye level with an advancing OR14. Luckily, Chase still has two smaller guns in her holster, as well as the laser cutter. Her hands find the butt of her gun now, and in one hard blow she brings it down on the head of the warbot. With the sound of tearing metal and shattered machinery, the omnic falls heavily into the server rack opposite. A couple of omnics on the other side are crushed with it, creating an opening for Chase to jump and take several swings at the access point. She just manages to finish it off with the laser cutter, then turns to find herself surrounded by omnics.

With her new, stronger body, she's exhilarated to discover that—even unarmed—she is finally a match for these machines. As she dodges hits, she thinks back to the start of the Crisis, to that day in the park. She wasn't much match for even the standard omnic model back then, and now she's able to go toe to toe with machines made for war. It gives her some measure of satisfaction and makes her hope that Liao, who has barely any combat training, can survive the fight.

In the server room, the OR14s were distracted, trying to keep the delicate machinery intact while fending off Chase. As soon as she's back outside, those same units crash down aisles and burst through walls with a terrifying groan of steel. With guns in both hands, Chase brute-forces her way back to the mezzanine. As soon as she gets there, a scream—a *human* scream—pierces the air.

Chase wouldn't have heard it if the factory wasn't so quiet. A couple of floors down, Liao is hanging off the edge of the mezzanine. The robotic arm of a piece of machinery is swinging wildly at her. Although she's flinching from being hit, below is a drop of almost ten stories, and by Chase's guess, she'll only be able to hold on for a couple more seconds.

How to save her?

Chase looks around, but the next maglift is a while away, and by the time she's circled the floors between herself and Liao, the woman could be dead. She needs to move fast. Chase looks around frantically, wondering if she can make the jump, but then her eye alights on the carbon-fiber column a couple of meters before her. Chase takes a running leap for it, misses with one arm, but manages to grab it with the other. Clinging to the column as tight as she can, she rides it two floors down, banging her hips and legs against it from the momentum. The friction burns the skin on her palms so badly, she thinks she can feel some of the silicone skin on her prostheses melt. She makes it down just in time to grab Liao, and they both fall heavily onto the second floor.

"Thank you," Liao breathes. She looks bruised by the fight and the fall.

Chase can see blood trickling down the side of her face behind her helmet.

"We need to disconnect the access point . . . They stopped me before I even got close."

They run toward it together, Chase leading the way but following Liao's directions. Holding the gun in her burned hands hurts, but she grits her teeth through the pain and continues forward.

When they reach the server room, all the omnic forces are focused on them.

"Get inside!" Chase shouts, positioning herself in front of the doorway. "Disable the access point while I hold them off!"

Chase fires a few rounds into the line of omnics, counting herself lucky that they won't risk shooting into the room and hitting the machinery. The doorway acts as a natural choke point, but even she won't be able to hold the room for long against a solid wall of Bastions.

"Done!" Liao practically screams.

Chase makes an attempt to keep up the fight, but her handguns are barely powerful enough to dent a single unit, and her laser cutter has been lost in the fray.

"We're trapped," Liao says, her voice tight.

Chase sees that she's right. Against these numbers, with limitless backup and resources, there's no possible way to fight their way out. It's only a matter of time before Chase tires or slips up. They won't be able to reach the final access point.

"Maybe Jack's made it," Liao says. There's a look in her eye, something in her tone that seems suddenly resigned to their fate.

And it's true. If he's made it to the final access point, their mission will still be a success, even if the two of them die here. They'll have given their lives for Canada—for the world. They'll have to hope that it's enough to make a difference in this fight, even if it means their story ends here.

A Bastion takes a swing for Chase and connects. Chase scrambles to her feet as the room is flooded by omnics. Another Bastion comes for her as Chase stands between the doctor and the omnic. Its heavy fist makes a dent in the wall behind them. Chase leans forward and pushes over one of the server racks, using all her might. It provides a temporary barricade between them and the robots, but it won't last for long.

"You know, I've just remembered . . . ," Liao says, looking around now as if she's lost something. "The building challenge with server rooms is always climate control."

Chase doesn't respond; she's aiming her precious few ammunition at a Bastion.

"Servers and computers generate a lot of heat, which can cause damage to the machinery. Anyone building a server room must consider how they will minimize hotspots by allowing"—she points up at the ceiling—"airflow."

"Brilliant, as always!" Chase laughs as she sees it too: an air vent!

Chase helps Liao climb up to it first. She clambers over the upturned server rack, finds purchase on another, pulls herself up and jumps, pushing the grate away. Chase boosts her up inside.

Liao turns and reaches a hand to help Chase up, and they wriggle free of the Bastions. The sounds of the factory seem to be amplified in the air vent.

The space is small, and for a little while Chase worries it's not strong enough to carry her heavy limbs, but the two of them manage to crawl through the darkness, toward another grate.

Liao presses her face against it and says, "It's the corridor outside. If we give it a minute, we might be able to jump down just as the maglift is coming. It will take us to the final server room."

"Let's do it."

Chase can hear the sound of gunfire on other floors, rocket explosions. *Jack,* she thinks, wondering if he's managed to disconnect his access point yet. *Is he okay? Is he heading to the final server?*

"Now!" Liao says. She pushes away the grate cover and leaps down. Chase rushes quickly after her and lands on the maglift with enough momentum to cause whiplash as they fly down to the next floor.

It's about seven revolutions around the massive factory before they reach the last long corridor. Jack is already there, Chase sees, but she enjoys only a moment of relief.

When her eyes adjust to the darkness, she sees the unblinking sensors of hundreds of warbots.

They're creatures she's never seen before, these menacing monsters the omnium has dreamed up in the dark. Tall humanoid robots reinforced with superhuman strength and speed, heavily armed. As soon as Chase and the doctor leap off the maglift, the omnics crash toward them.

Chase fires her guns—the last of her ammunition—vaulting away from mechanical arms and the path of weapons. Jack fires helix rockets into the melee; it slows them a little, but not by much. Chase is about to dive through their legs, hoping to slalom to the server room. Behind her she hears Liao cry out with a bone-chilling scream.

It's only when she turns that she sees what the doctor is shouting at. A helix rocket arcs through the air and hits a bundle of canisters that read PRESSURIZED OXYGEN.

Chase's blood turns to ice. All of them duck for cover as a colossal explosion tears through the room. Their bodies are tossed against the far wall with enough force to shatter bone. For a little while, Chase's vision goes black.

When she manages to open her eyes, she feels as if she's woken up at the end of a party, and scrap metal bits of robots are littered like piñata shells across the floor. Liao is on the ground too, and Jack is frantically checking her pulse, taking off her helmet.

"Is she . . ."

Chase opens her mouth to say *alive*, but she can't hear anything at all. Nothing but a white noise whining in her ear. Jack shakes his head. Mouths something.

The access point, Chase thinks. They still need to get to it. The hall that leads to the final server room is blocked by a bright wall of flames. *Impossible to reach it now*, she thinks, but when she looks back at Jack he's pointing to it, moving his lips, though she can't hear him.

You, she thinks she can read from them. *You. Only you can do it.*

Can she, though? It's true that Chase's body can withstand higher temperatures, and the filters in her lungs mean that she won't die so quickly of smoke inhalation. But that doesn't change the fact that Chase is terrified. It's one thing walking into probable death, but another thing to override all her evolutionary impulses and stride into a blazing fire.

You, the word she thinks she sees on Jack's mouth.

Chase's limbs won't let her do it, though. No part of her body. Billowing pillars of smoke are flying up in huge gouts, filling the upper floor, the ceilings. Jack is bent double coughing, his eyes streaming already.

Chase thinks about the days after she was diagnosed, when the doctors gave her mere weeks to live. Back then, she would stare at her twin's healthy body and wonder what twist of fate had chosen her, alone. A reflexive thing inside her to ask *why*.

Would it be easier if you had an answer? her grandmother replied once.

Of course! Chase cried, *This has to mean something!*

What if it meant nothing at all? Everything she's been through—the triumphs, the pain, the adjustments—then and now, to get here?

Make it mean something, her grandmother told her. *Maybe, you get to choose.*

Chase looks down at her friction-burnt hand. The loose way

the silicone skin is hanging off it now, the flicker and flash of her metal bones underneath: metacarpals, phalanges, 3D-printed tendons. When Liao gave her these enhancements, she'd seen them as her strength, but was it?

Or was it her sharp mind, honed during years in and out of that hospital bed, even then battling these machines who now want to turn her world to ash. Or her tolerance for pain, won from countless procedures. Or the fact that even now, she's still standing, still has courage in the face of death … after staring it down her entire life.

She'll do it. Dash headlong into the inferno and not turn back. Because this is who she is.

Chase rushes past the burning bodies of omnics, twisted and melting over the soot-stained floor. Flames lick the walls, the doors, the railings. To get into the server room she needs to turn the handle, and when she does her silicone skin comes off like tenderized meat on a skewer.

She cries out in pain, but nobody can hear her. It's not so much pain as it would have been in her old body.

Inside the server room, blistering air is already blowing up through the vents, fire laps at the ceiling, wires flicker and throw sparks. The air smells of ozone, burnt electronics, evaporated hydraulic fluid, her own roasted flesh.

By the time she reaches the access point, there are error codes rolling across her vision, the edges of her mouth are blistered, and every breath flays her throat. Dismantling the final access point is the last thing she does before collapsing to the floor.

9

DETROIT

"Human or omnic?" a voice says. Chase wakes in the medevac vehicle, with sirens wailing above her. There's a sound of quiet frustration, and when Chase opens her eyes, she sees a doctor in a US Army uniform.

"Sorry," she says, deactivating the scanner at the end of the bed. "Those things never work well enough on augmented hearts." Then, with a sigh, "We're moving on—is it too much to ask that all our tech moves on with us?"

Chase would have smiled if it didn't hurt so much. There's an oxygen mask attached to her face. Apparently she inhaled enough smoke to damage the filter on her lungs. "Not permanently," the doctor reassures her. "At least, in the cybernetics wing of our hospital, we can mend it." She looks a little sadly at the rest of Chase. "And everything else."

When she holds a hand up in front of her eyes, she sees that her skin and tendons have completely melted off their metal frame.

"Dr. Liao? Jack?" she asks.

"Right here," comes a rasp behind her, and with some effort she turns to find them both on different stretchers. Liao has an oxygen mask on her face, tinfoil blankets wrapped around her shoulders. Her eyes are closed, but she gives a thumbs-up.

Chase exhales with relief. "We . . . did it?"

"We did," they both say.

There's a metallic tone then, over the comms on the medevac van. A holoscreen pops up, and Torbjörn's face appears.

"Glad to see you all awake," he says. "We're evacuating you for treatment, but I wanted to give you the good news myself. The omnium halted production and deployment of new units when the last access point was destroyed."

"The new Titans?" Chase manages to get out.

Captain Page from the US Army comes into focus behind Torbjörn. "We've managed to secure backup. We have a couple of battalions on their way to finish the job. Destroy the last of the warbots in this area and dismantle the factory."

"Turns out," Torbjörn tells them, "Chase and Liao's theory was right. This omnium was being controlled from outside."

"What?" Chase wheezes, her mind reeling at the implications. "Who—?"

"Liao's team will be focusing all their efforts on finding out," he says. "Now that she's being formally brought into Overwatch."

"What about . . . ?" Chase asks. The display on her retina

shows her the position of some of her troops, but she needs to know if they're okay. Who will live and who will keep fighting.

"They succeeded in their mission," Jack says. "But it came at a cost."

Captain Page reads off the numbers of lost and wounded. Chase is relieved to hear that Noah survived, though he's in another medevac van, along with Sergeants Avery, Harper, and Camille. Chase is saddened by the losses, but she's never felt prouder of her team. Thanks to their sacrifice, the world has a fighting chance.

When the other commanding officers join the call moments later, it sounds as if there's a rowdy party going on back at the base.

"Well done, Captain Chase," says Commanding Officer Fournier.

Chase struggles to salute.

"At ease, soldier. The duty you and your team performed for your country today won't soon be forgotten."

"A cheer for Captain Vivian Chase!" a lower-ranking officer shouts. In the background, someone makes a joke about getting out the champagne.

Chase can hardly hear the rest of what Fournier is saying for the sound all around her. Seashell resonance. Blood crashing through her ears. Everyone is cheering, clapping. Calling her by her bunk name.

"To Sojourn!"

"Needless to say, the team here is excited to welcome you back," says Fournier. "I'll be paying you a personal visit myself upon your return. See you soon, Captain."

The call cuts out, and Chase relaxes onto the gurney.

"We make a great team." Jack laughs, pulling off his oxygen mask to grin. It seemed impossible, just the three of them against a city full of omnics.

He turns to her now, more serious. "You know," he says, "that offer to join Overwatch still stands. The team could use your expert tactics, your strength. You could do a lot of good for the world."

Chase smiles inwardly at it but shakes her head.

"Maybe one day," she says. "Right now, my country still needs me."

EPILOGUE

TORONTO

She's had dreams lovely as this. They're back on Centre Island, eight months since the attack began, in a memorial garden where the summer-flowering plants are flourishing. Violet starbursts of allium, black-eyed Susans, fistfuls of hydrangeas, heady-smelling cones of sweet lilac, daisies heavy with bees. It's a bright day, with only a few cirrus clouds floating high in the atmosphere, wispy contrails lit amber. Toronto's skyline is forever changed, but life is going on, everywhere. Although the war is still raging, they've managed to take this city back. New things are being dug out and rebuilt from the rubble: homes, museums, gardens. And people too—the people are recovering.

It's the kind of day Vivian Chase feared she would never see again at the start of the Crisis. Their attack on the Detroit omnium gave Canada a much needed break. Once they quarantined the factory, the US Army were called in to finish the job and shut the omnium down. Liao stayed behind to instruct the military on the dismantlement. With the dent to omnic production, the CAF and the US military were able to launch their long campaign of attacks. Through a process of slow attrition, they were able to take back and secure many of the cities. There are still battles to fight before the war has its final hour—and Chase hopes to see her people through as many of them as she can.

The mission proved Dr. Liao to be an essential voice in the fight for humanity. A couple of months after their success in Detroit, Liao was formally inducted into Overwatch, a move that was welcomed by the whole strike team, though perhaps none more so than Torbjörn.

This afternoon is Bonnie's sixth birthday. Chase and Valentine join happily in as their laughing friends and relatives sing to her. Chase has spent so long hoping for this day that—watching her niece's jubilant face, bathed in birthday cake candlelight—it takes on an almost dreamlike quality.

Bonnie blows out her candles, and everyone cheers. Valentine, in a bright-yellow maternity sundress, helps to cut into the fondant, and then the group disperses. Their father starts to lead his amateur brass quartet in a jazzy rendition of "Happy Birthday." Their mother and Bonnie's father begin ushering sticky-fingered children to another activity. Chase and Valentine retreat to man the cake table, wearing gold party hats, watching everything from a slight distance and enjoying the heady smell of sugar coming off the cookies and cotton candy.

Bonnie and a couple of her friends, children in bright dresses and wielding flowing streamers, begin chasing one another in and out of the trick fountains. The water makes arcing rainbows of light spray across the park, hissing on the hot stone pavement.

"She loves how much faster she is than the other children." Valentine laughs, brimming with pride. "She feels as if she's got a superpower."

"She has," Chase says. Valentine told her that Bonnie chose her pink chiffon dress specifically to show off her new cybernetic legs. It was a long recovery for her, months in and out of the hospital, but now she's come out the other side.

"You know what she told me the other day? That she's hoping to grow up to be just like her auntie." Valentine smiles at her sister. "I hope so too. I hope that growing up with her new body will make her fearless but compassionate, empathetic and forgiving. Like you."

Chase bats away a sherbet-colored balloon gusting toward her. She takes a spoonful of cake, a vanilla sponge with Bonnie's current favorite cartoon character printed on the icing. "It's been so long," Chase says with a smile at the sweetness of the icing, "since I've had cake."

"I got your package in the mail," Valentine says, holding out her left hand. Chase's attention falls to their grandmother's ring.

"I'm glad it finally got back to you."

"Thank you," Valentine says. "For finding it. For keeping it safe. I know it's little in the scheme of things, but it's so dear to me." She looks at it intently now, as she might a watch face.

"I'm sorry it took so long. I had to get the stone replaced." The last time Chase remembers looking at it, the milky opal was like a missing tooth. A sorry sight, since she remembers how much their grandmother loved it, and Valentine too.

"You know, when I first got it, I felt pretty bad about how damaged it was. Mum cheered me up about it. She said that opals are pretty soft stones, and Grandma had to get them replaced a couple of times when she was alive."

Chase didn't know that, though she remembers that before Valentine's wedding it was in such bad shape they'd had to commission a jeweler to replace all the worn gold prongs.

"It's like the ship of Theseus," Chase says. "The sails were replaced, and then eventually the hull. Was it still the same ship?"

A slight breeze picks up and tosses biodegradable confetti in little eddies across the cobbled path.

"Yes," Valentine says, stroking her left hand contemplatively. The opal does look pretty in the light, capturing rainbow splinters of it. "I loved Grandma, and she gave me this wedding gift . . . It doesn't matter what it's made of. What matters is that I love it."

Chase smiles, and Valentine puts her paper plate down on the table. "So, this is also my way of trying to say . . . that I'm sorry."

"For what?"

"For that thing I said, the first day of the Crisis. The day that Bonnie was hurt. The thing I said about you not having a 'real' heart." Her sister winces now, as if repeating the words is causing her physical pain. Chase flinches too at them, remembering how hurt she was, and for how long.

"I shouldn't have said it," Valentine admits. "I was upset. I was . . ." She sighs, her eyes drifting back to the party. Bonnie and her friends are playing with a bubble machine, their laughter floating across the garden. "And anyway," she says finally, "I shouldn't have said it because it wasn't true."

She reaches out a warm hand and touches Chase's chest, lets her palm fall on her titanium rib cage. If Chase is very still, she sometimes thinks she can hear the whoosh of blood through the silicone chambers of it.

"I love your heart," Valentine says. "Because it brought you back to me."

ABOUT THE AUTHOR

TEMI OH wrote her first novel while studying for a BSci in neuroscience. Her degree provided great opportunities to write and learn about topics ranging from philosophy of the mind to space physiology. While at university, Temi founded a book club called Neuroscience-fiction, where she led discussions about science-fiction books that focus on the brain. After she received an MA in creative writing from the University of Edinburgh, her first novel, *Do You Dream of Terra-Two?*, was published by Simon & Schuster. It won the American Library Association's Alex Award in 2020 and was an NPR Best Book of the year in 2019. Her short stories have been published by Flame Tree Press and in *Black Panther: Tales of Wakanda*. Her second novel, *More Perfect*, will be published by Simon & Schuster in 2023.

WRITTEN BY:
TEMI OH

COVER ILLUSTRATED BY:
MANDELA SMITH

EDITED BY:
CHLOE FRABONI

DESIGNED BY:
COREY PETERSCHMIDT AND JESSICA RODRIGUEZ

PRODUCED BY:
BRIANNE MESSINA

LORE CONSULTATION BY:
MADI BUCKINGHAM

GAME TEAM CONSULTATION BY:
**JEFF CHAMBERLAIN, GAVIN JURGENS-FYHRIE,
AARON KELLER, DION ROGERS, ARNOLD TSANG**

SPECIAL THANKS:
GLEN CHI, ANGEL GIUFFRIA

BLIZZARD ENTERTAINMENT

VICE PRESIDENT, CONSUMER PRODUCTS: **MATTHEW BEECHER**
DIRECTOR, CONSUMER PRODUCTS, PUBLISHING: **BYRON PARNELL**
ASSOCIATE PUBLISHING MANAGER: **DEREK ROSENBERG**
DIRECTOR, MANUFACTURING: **ANNA WAN**
SENIOR DIRECTOR, STORY AND
FRANCHISE DEVELOPMENT: **DAVID SEEHOLZER**
SENIOR PRODUCER: **BRIANNE MESSINA**
LEAD EDITOR: **CHLOE FRABONI**
SENIOR EDITOR: **ELANA COHEN**
SENIOR EDITOR: **ERIC GERON**
BOOK ART & DESIGN MANAGER: **COREY PETERSCHMIDT**
HISTORIAN SUPERVISOR: **SEAN COPELAND**
SENIOR HISTORIAN: **JUSTIN PARKER**
ASSOCIATE HISTORIAN: **MADI BUCKINGHAM**

For more fantastic fiction, author events,
exclusive excerpts, competitions, limited editions and more

VISIT OUR WEBSITE
titanbooks.com

LIKE US ON FACEBOOK
facebook.com/titanbooks

FOLLOW US ON TWITTER AND INSTAGRAM
@TitanBooks

EMAIL US
readerfeedback@titanemail.com